m.e.j.

EUGENIA

Also Available in Large Print
by Clare Darcy

Regina
Elyza
Lady Pamela

EUGENIA

Clare Darcy

G.K.HALL &CO.

 Boston, Massachusetts

1978

Library of Congress Cataloging in Publication Data

Darcy, Clare.
  Eugenia.

  "Large print ed."
  1. Large type books. I. Title.
[PZ4.D2145Eu 1978] [PS3554.A67] 813'.5'4 77-29205
ISBN 0-8161-6576-9

Published in Large Print by arrangement with Walker
and Company

Set in Photon 18 Pt Crown

EUGENIA

CHAPTER

1

On a bright morning near the close of the month of May in the year 1811 an elegant travelling-chaise, with a crest upon the panel, drew up before Miss Bascom's Select Academy for Young Ladies in Queen Square, Bath. The chaise, which belonged to that eminent peer and statesman, the Earl of Chandross, was well known in Queen Square, where it had arrived punctually on every occasion during the past three years when the Earl's young cousin and ward, Miss Eugenia Liddiard, had gone to spend her holidays at Mere Court, the Earl's principal seat in Essex; and on this occasion, which was to be its last appearance in the Square, Miss Bascom herself had condescended to speed Miss Liddiard upon her way by accompanying her to its door.

Not, it must be stated, in compliment to Miss Liddiard. Miss Liddiard herself, to Miss Bascom's certain knowledge, was a very small cog indeed in the very large wheel of the Earl's interests, and, beyond paying his ward's fees with admirable promptness, his lordship — and, for that matter, her ladyship as well — had evinced not the least degree of concern for her over the period during which she had been a boarder at Miss Bascom's establishment. She had been sent to Miss Bascom's chiefly, Miss Bascom suspected, because there was no niche either at Mere Court or in his lordship's magnificent town house in Grosvenor Square into which a half-formed schoolgirl of independent character and unpredictable inclinations would properly fit, and Miss Bascom, after three years of unremitting effort to shape her into the sort of young female who *would* fit into such a niche, was obliged to admit that she had dismally failed.

It was to be hoped, Miss Bascom not very sanguinely thought as she surveyed Miss Liddiard's slender, chip-hatted and duffle-cloaked figure descending the steps of the Select Academy, that some eligible gentleman would miraculously appear in the course of the forthcoming London Season, during which she was to be "brought out" by Lady Chandross, and marry her out of hand; for decidedly young Miss Liddiard was in no way suited to life in a great house as a poor dependant upon her noble relations.

Miss Liddiard herself, who was engaged in making her adieux to her greatest friend, Miss Amelia Rowntree, known to her schoolfellows as Muffet, appeared at the moment to be not in the least depressed by a sense of her own shortcomings. On the contrary, she looked uncommonly cheerful, and her vivid, handsome little face, with its well-arched brows, mobile mouth, and elegant nose set beneath a gloriously untidy mane of dark silky hair that fell over her shoulders almost to her waist, was glowing as she and Miss Rowntree discussed their plans for meeting again in London a week or two hence. Muffet, a small, fair, rather plain girl, was a friend of happier days, when Eugenia had lived with her father in Kent on a small but very satisfactory estate called Coverts that had adjoined Squire Rowntree's acres there, and she and Muffet and Muffet's older brother Tom had been as inseparable then as a litter of puppies, and had played and quarrelled and romped together with the same equable abandon.

Muffet, who was less enterprising than her friend, had always regarded her with a kind of hero-worshipping devotion, which had deepened almost to awe as Eugenia, shipped off to Mere Court upon her father's death three years before, had subsequently swum once more into her ken at Miss Bascom's, full of casual titbits about that enormous and celebrated mansion and the excitements of living in the orbit of the most famous names in the London *ton*. Prinny (for so, Eugenia informed her, the Prince of Wales, now the Prince Regent, was known

4

to his intimates) had stayed at Mere Court; Lady Jersey, Lord Alvanley, "Cupid" Palmerston, and the Seftons were frequent visitors; and upon one memorable occasion she had even come across Mr. Brummell, the famous Beau himself, in one of the corridors, and had had the distinction of being looked through by him with all his inimitable hauteur.

This, to Muffet, whose most *recherche* diversions had been an occasional visit to Canterbury and her journeys to and from Miss Bascom's Academy in Bath, was bliss beyond dreams; but Eugenia took it all very coolly and said she would give it up in a minute for a chance to go back to Kent and live at Coverts again. This being highly improbable, as Coverts was now the property of her father's cousin, Cedric Liddiard, a very scholarly clergyman and a confirmed bachelor, who, upon inheriting it, had continued to reside in the Cathedral Close in Canterbury and had left it entirely in the hands of an agent, she and Muffet had recently concocted a plan in which she was to marry Muffet's brother Tom, after which they would all live together in Kent for the rest of their lives in perfect happiness.

Of course Tom, who considered Eugenia a very good sort of girl but, at nineteen, was far more interested in country sports than in marrying, had not heard of these plans as yet, and might have some rather strenuous objections to them when he did. But this was as nothing and less than nothing to Eugenia, who considered obstacles only as things to be surmounted, and who had informed Muffet the night before that if she did not wish to sound Tom out on the subject of rather immediate matrimony, she, Eugenia, would write and propose the plan to him herself.

"But you can't do *that!*" Muffet, scandalised, had said, curling up on Eugenia's bed and tucking her feet under her, looking, as she did so, very young indeed in her high-necked, prettily ruffled nightdress, with her fair hair emerging from beneath the nightcap of fine muslin firmly tied beneath her chin.

"Why not?" Eugenia asked.

"It — it wouldn't be proper! To propose

marriage to a gentleman —"

"Pooh! It isn't a *gentleman*. It's only Tom."

"Yes, but —" Muffet had protested, clutching Eugenia's pillow to her young and meagre bosom as if for protection against her friend's alarming directness upon a matter that she had been taught must be approached with suitable maidenly reserve.

"And, what is more," Eugenia had said, alarming her still further, "it's not as if he won't be able to do just as he likes when we are married. Gussie" (this, Muffet knew, was Augusta, Lady Chandross, who had petrified her with admiration, upon the single occasion she had seen her, when she had been taken for a treat to Drury Lane Theatre on her way home to Kent for the Christmas holidays, by appearing in her box in a diaphanous gown that had clung so perfectly to her excessively slender figure that it would have delighted an anatomist intent upon counting all her bones) "Gussie," Eugenia continued, "says it is very unfashionable for a wife to interfere with her husband's *petits plaisirs*, and I am sure I have no intention of doing so."

"Oh, *Eugenia!*" said Muffet, pink with admiring embarrassment at her friend's grown-upness. "But Tom *wouldn't,* you know! He is not at all in the petticoat line! Indeed, I don't think he will *quite* like being married, even to you."

Which statement caused Eugenia to remark, in a very *un*grown-up way, that she couldn't see what difference it would make to him whether he was married or not, and if he meant to be mulish about it, she would simply have to arrange somehow to go down to Kent and talk to him herself.

The matter had then been left in abeyance, and as the presence of Miss Bascom now, and of the abigail sent by Lady Chandross to chaperon Eugenia upon her journey, somewhat inhibited the parting words the two friends were able to exchange, Eugenia was obliged to depart without any very clear understanding's having been reached between them on the matter of how it was to be arranged for her to become Mrs. Thomas Rowntree in the near future.

The chaise steps having been put up and the door shut by the liveried postillion, the chaise at last rolled away from Miss Bascom's Select Academy, leaving its proprietress uttering a mental, "Thank goodness!" and Muffet, who was not a sentimental girl but felt that life would be sadly flat without her friend's enlivening presence, stifling an inclination to sniffle. As for Eugenia herself, she settled back upon the luxurious claret-velvet squabs of the chaise beside the middle-aged abigail, whose name was Trimmer, and prepared to enjoy to the full all the experiences that might present themselves to one during a journey of some hundred and twenty-five miles upon a fine day in May.

Unfortunately, the day remained fine only as far as the Wiltshire border, for as the chaise began to climb Box Hill, clouds were already rolling in from the west, and in a very short time rain began to fall. Eugenia, always an optimist, was sure it would clear by the time they reached Calne; when they halted at Beckhampton Inn and partook of a nuncheon of prawns, peas, and apple tarts in a coffeeroom with its windows dismally flooded with pelting drops, she was convinced it must soon come on to be fair; and when Trimmer, her nerves quite overset in late afternoon by the continued downpour and the gloomy predictions of the postillions that the road would be found to be washed out beneath them if they proceeded further, suggested that they stop for the night at the King's Head in Thatcham, instead of going on to the more prestigious Pelican in Speenhamland, where they were expected, she said tolerantly that she was quite willing to do so, because she had never stopped at the King's Head, so that it was bound to be more interesting than the Pelican, but added that it seemed a bit silly to her to be daunted by a little rain.

This description of the weather might have appeared a trifle inadequate to an unprejudiced observer, in view of the torrents now being poured upon an already sodden landscape by the lowering skies overhead, but Eugenia continued to ignore its depressing qualities, as the chaise drew up before the door of the

King's Head, by running through the downpour in advance of the landlord's umbrella, which had hastened out to meet her with the landlord himself beneath it. Arriving inside the inn, she shook the raindrops from her cloak and looked about her with a general air of approval.

And, indeed, the sight of well-polished brasses and a large oak settle with a black-and-white kitten comfortably asleep upon its cushions, and a glimpse through an open doorway into a snug coffeeroom where several guests were enjoying what appeared to be raised pigeon pies and mushroom fritters, were enough to have cheered the heart of any wayfarer. Eugenia, responding with enthusiasm to the landlord's enquiry as to what he might do for her, said she would like a bedchamber for herself and an adjoining one for her maid.

"A nice featherbed without any lumps, if you have got one, and simply lashings of food. I am frightfully hungry!" she added; upon which the landlord, who had taken in the crest, the elegant chaise, and the abigail in the wink of an eye and was therefore content to overlook the carelessly worn schoolgirl hat and the young lady's entire lack of any pretensions to à la modality, said obsequiously that she should have his best bedchamber and a private parlour, to which an excellent dinner prepared by Mrs. Landlord herself would shortly be borne.

Eugenia, who liked new experiences of any sort, looked regretfully at the coffeeroom, which indubitably offered far greater scope for the indulgence of a free-ranging curiosity than did the prospect of a meal taken abovestairs in a private parlour, with only Trimmer in attendance, but decided against pressing the point because of the fuss that would be made on all sides. It would, she considered, be a further advantage in marrying Tom that no one except a husband was permitted to tell a married lady what she must do, and she had not the least doubt about Tom's being agreeable to letting her do whatever she liked.

Trimmer having now arrived at the inn

door as well, with many injunctions to the servants who were bringing in the portmanteaux, Eugenia was prepared to follow the landlord up the stairs at the rear of the lobby when the door opened once more on a gust of blowing rain and three passengers from the Bristol and Bath Accommodation-coach, which had driven into the inn-yard just behind the chaise, entered the passage. All were very wet, their coats darkened with damp and rain dripping in little rivulets from their hat brims, by which telltale signs the landlord was able to set them down at once as outside passengers and therefore unworthy of his personal attention.

Eugenia, glancing over her shoulder to survey them with equable interest as she set her foot upon the lowest step of the staircase, saw a dejected-looking middle-aged man who might have been a clerk, a burly farmer in stout, muddy boots and a brass-buttoned coat — and then her eyes fell upon the third passenger, a dark, enigmatic-looking young man in his middle twenties, with a faintly arrogant air that, taken in conjunction with his

13

distinctly shabby olive-green coat, gave him rather the air of a gentleman who had come down in the world.

"Gerry!" she cried on the instant, recognising her cousin, Gerald Liddiard, who, like herself, was one of Lord Chandross's encumbrances, and who, as he was possessed of some eight or nine years' seniority over her, an even more urgent desire for new experiences, and the advantage of being of the male sex, had already caused the Earl far more trouble and expense than she herself had ever dreamed of doing. She turned about abruptly, thus causing Trimmer, who was close behind her, to fall back in some disarray.

The three newly arrived passengers also gazed at her in slight surprise, each then glancing at the others to see which of them was being thus addressed, the young man in the olive-green coat appearing the least interested of them all, however, as if he could not conceive how the matter could have anything to do with him. He was a very bronzed young man, with the lithe figure and easy movements of one who had spent a great deal of his time in outdoor pursuits, but just now he appeared extremely pale, and his dark eyes had an overbright look that a medical man would instantly have diagnosed as being due to fever.

''Gerry!'' said Eugenia again impatiently, and this time it was apparent to them all that she was addressing the young man in the olive-green coat. "Don't you know me? It's Eugenia —''

The young man looked at her with a politely disinterested air, shrugged his shoulders slightly, and turned away towards the door of the coffeeroom. Eugenia looked at him in astonishment. She had not seen her cousin for almost three years, as after having been sent down from Oxford, he had embarked upon an adventurous career that appeared to leave him very little time for his relations, whose chief communication with him had been in the form of letters urgently requesting them to settle some of his more pressing debts; and she was aware that three years had made rather drastic alterations in her own appearance.

Still it was the outside of enough, she considered, when one's own cousin, who had spent most of his holidays at Coverts before her father had died and whom one had known since one had been in short coats, failed to recognise one and was, it appeared, about to cut one dead.

She laid a detaining hand upon the young man's arm.

"Really, Gerry," she said, "how *can* you be so stupid! I know it has been three years, but still —"

By this time Trimmer, who was by no means an old retainer, familiar with family ramifications, having been engaged from a London Registry Office by Lady Chandross only some two weeks before, projected herself into the scene, and with a scandalised exclamation of, "Now, miss, if you please!" attempted to draw her away. She had been warned by Lady Chandross that she would find her young charge an odd, forward girl, whom it would be her duty to keep out of the briars into which, given the least opportunity, she was all too prone to fall; but not in her wildest flights of fancy had she imagined Miss Liddiard's going so far as to attempt to scrape acquaintance with an obviously uninterested young man who had apparently never seen her before in his life.

"Now, miss, really —!" she expostulated. "Indeed, you must not —"

"Oh, Trimmer, *do* be quiet!" said Eugenia, maintaining her hold upon the young man's arm. "It is *quite* all right; he is my cousin. I have known him all my life. And if you don't care even to speak to me," she went on, addressing the young man, "very well! I daresay this is your notion of a joke —"

The young man, looking somewhat enlightened by the explanatory part of this speech, though it had been addressed to Trimmer and not to himself, said politely at this point, "I am afraid you are making a mistake, you know. I am not your cousin."

Eugenia looked at him, drawing her brows together in a slight, puzzled frown.

"But you are! You must be!" she argued. "I can't be mistaken!"

"Still I am afraid you are," the young

man said, pleasantly but definitely, and moved on towards the door of the coffeeroom.

Eugenia looked after him with a disapproving expression upon her face.

"Oh!" she said. "If that isn't just like Gerry, to play such a trick on one! And ten to one he will come knocking on my door in half an hour, expecting me to laugh over it with him!"

"But, my dear Miss Liddiard," fluttered Trimmer, looking askance at the clerk, the farmer, and the landlord, who had taken in the entire scene with the greatest interest and were still standing with their mouths acock, "are you *quite* sure —? After all, if it has been some time since you have seen your cousin —"

Eugenia said definitely that she was completely sure, and, gathering her cloak about her, was preparing once more to mount the stairs when she was again interrupted by a sudden commotion from beyond the coffeeroom door. Without hesitation she turned about, walked into the coffeeroom, and beheld a pair of astonished waiters regarding the unconscious form of the young man in the olive-green coat, which lay slumped upon the floor.

"I thought so," she said briefly. "Fever, I expect." She turned to the landlord, who had followed her into the room. "This is my cousin, Mr. Gerald Liddiard," she said. "I expect he has been ill, and, as you see, he has fainted. Will you have him carried up to a bedchamber, please, and send at once for a doctor?"

The landlord, who was not accustomed to taking his orders from schoolgirls, looked doubtfully at Trimmer. She looked back at him with an equally dubious gaze, but as Eugenia was now engaged in supervising the attempts of the two waiters to carry the recumbent young man's six-foot form out of the coffeeroom and up the stairs, it was really of very little importance, it seemed, whether they approved or not. They trailed out of the coffeeroom after the stumbling waiters, and at the head of the stairs the landlord, succumbing to Eugenia's imperatively questioning gaze, opened a door just off the landing and led the little procession inside.

"You can put him down here," he said rather gloomily to the waiters, for, crest or no crest, he was far from certain that young Miss Liddiard's travel allowance was sufficiently large to cover a surgeon's fee and an additional bedchamber, and the young man's definitely threadbare coat did not speak of prosperity.

But under his young guest's cool hazel-green eyes he hardly liked somehow to put his doubts into words, and went off, muttering to himself about a "hem queer setout," to send a boy to fetch the doctor and a chambermaid to bring some hartshorn, this also by Eugenia's orders.

Meanwhile, Eugenia, after instructing the waiters to pull off the young man's boots and remove his coat, herself loosened his cravat and tucked him up efficiently beneath the patchwork quilt that lay upon the bed. She then wetted her handkerchief in the yellow ware jug on the washstand, applied it to his brow, and, taking one of his hands, began to chafe it between her own, instructing the agitated Trimmer to do the same with the other.

"But, my dear Miss Liddiard, are you quite, *quite* sure it really *is* your cousin?" Trimmer twittered once more, taking in an exceedingly gingerly fashion the bronzed hand that lay limp upon the coverlet. "Only think how dreadful it would be if it were not! A perfectly strange young man — I do not know *what* Lady Chandross will think if I have permitted you to enter a strange man's bedchamber —!"

"She won't think anything at all about it if you don't tell her," Eugenia said practically. "Besides, it *is* Gerry. I am quite sure of it. I expect we shall have to take him back to Mere with us, for it looks very much to me as if his pockets were to let, and he has certainly been quite ill. I wonder what he has been doing with himself. It has been almost a year since anyone has heard from him, and then he was in some sort of trouble in Cheltenham over an heiress he tried to run off with."

Trimmer shuddered, and with a start dropped the hand she had been chafing.

"Oh, you needn't worry; he didn't succeed," Eugenia said kindly. "It is rather a pity in a way, though, that he didn't, because he hasn't any money except what Lord Chandross gives him, and it would have made things so much more comfortable for him, wouldn't it? And he *has* a great deal of charm, so she would have had *some*thing for her money." She looked critically at the young man's face, where a touch of colour had begun to creep into the pale cheeks. "He is coming round, I think," she said. "Do see if you can hurry that girl with the hartshorn, Trimmer — or, better still, go and fetch your own. I daresay you have some by you."

Trimmer, impressed by the competence with which her young mistress was dealing with the patient, went reluctantly away, quite unaware that she was merely the latest in a long series of servants whom Eugenia, cast from childhood in the role of companion and guide to her cheerful, reckless father by her mother's early death, had dragooned or cajoled into doing what was needed for the helpless male creature currently requiring her care. Eugenia continued to chafe the young man's hands, and in a few moments was rewarded by seeing his eyes open and fix themselves with a vague, puzzled look upon her face.

"You fainted," she informed him. "You've been ill, I expect. Fever?"

"Yes," he said, in automatic response. "But I'm all right now."

"You will be, I daresay, if you take proper care of yourself," Eugenia said practically. "I don't know what you are up to or where you are intending to go now, Gerry, but if you have the least degree of sense you'll come to Mere with me and let yourself be looked after until you're in better frame."

The young man, obviously still gathering his wits together from the mists of unconsciousness, frowned slightly as he apparently recalled the scene downstairs.

"I haven't the least notion who you are, you know," he said after a moment, in his cool, lazy, agreeable voice, attempting to raise himself from his recumbent position and finding himself at once firmly restrained by a light hand upon his chest.

A shade of impatience crossed

Eugenia's face.

"Oh, Gerry, *don't* begin that again —" she said, and then halted abruptly, a slight uncertainty appearing in her eyes as she scanned the young man's face. "I'm Eugenia — Eugenia Liddiard, of course," she said rather hesitantly, after a moment. "Your cousin —"

She paused once more. The young man's expression had changed as she had spoken the name; a slight flush came into his bronzed face.

"Liddiard," he said slowly. "Yes, I expect that explains it."

"Explains what?"

"Your thinking I was related to you. I daresay in a way I am. That is, if a man named Charles Liddiard was your relation, too."

"Charles Liddiard?" The look of puzzlement deepened upon Eugenia's face. "*Charles* Liddiard? Why, yes. He was my father's first cousin, but he's been dead for ages. Before I was born. What has that to do —?"

"I'm his son. Richard Liddiard."

"Oh!" Eugenia, who had been sitting on

24

the bed, got up and backed away a little. "But Charles Liddiard," she said, "never —" and then coloured up and bit the sentence off short.

"He never married, and so I've no right to his name?" the young man said pleasantly. "They've told you that, I daresay — Chandross, your father, all the rest of the Liddiards —"

He was sitting up now, his feet swung over the side of the bed, and Eugenia, recovering herself, said to him firmly, "You had much better lie down. You'll only go off again if you try to get up too soon."

He sent a quick, rather quizzical glance at her from under his black brows.

"Well," Eugenia said reasonably, divining the cause of his surprise, "you really *are* just as much my cousin as Gerry is if you are Cousin Charles's son, aren't you? — whether he was ever married or not. So I expect I had as well stay and see that you are properly taken care of."

"Your relations," the young man said dryly, "might not share your solicitude."

"No, I daresay they wouldn't. They wouldn't care much what happened to Gerry, though, either, as long as he wasn't doing anything to disgrace the Liddiard name, so *that* doesn't make any difference, you see. You really are amazingly like him," she added, surveying the dark face with its strongly marked black brows, cleft chin, and general appearance of arrogant distinction as he lay back upon the pillows once more with an unwilling air of exhaustion. "I wonder you have never been taken for him before. Have you been living in England?"

"No. In Ireland."

"That accounts for it, I expect. I don't think Gerry has ever been in Ireland — though of course one never knows, because he seems to move about quite a bit."

"Is he a bad lot?"

"I expect people would say so. Cecil — that is my cousin, Lord Chandross, you know — certainly thinks he is, but I don't know that he's done anything particularly disgraceful, if you don't count gaming and fighting and not wanting to settle down and be what Cecil calls a credit to the family. He is very expensive, of course. You wouldn't believe how much he has cost Cecil, first and last." A faint shade of bitterness crossed the dark face on the pillows.

"Oh, I think I would," said the young man. "You see, I've heard what a handsome sum he was preparing to settle upon my mother if she would take herself and Charles Liddiard's brat quietly out of the way and be content to forget she was Charles Liddiard's wife. The Liddiards are extremely generous to their by-blows, I've been given to understand. They don't take quite so kindly to a misalliance."

Eugenia considered this. "No, I daresay they don't," she said after a moment. "Do you mean that Charles Liddiard really did marry your mother, only Cecil prefers to think that he didn't? But can't you prove —?"

"No," said the young man baldly. "My mother lived only a few months after I was born. Charles Liddiard died several months before that. He'd taken her to the

Continent, and in the confusion after her death her papers were lost. An English clergyman named Castle took me in charge and brought me up; he'd never seen either Charles Liddiard or my mother before in his life, and all he knew about me was the completely unconfirmed bit of information he was able to get from my mother before she died."

Eugenia thoughtfully digested this statement, and if the young man upon the bed had been observing her — which he was not, for he had closed his eyes as he had finished speaking, apparently feeling a return of the disagreeable faintness that had caused his collapse in the coffeeroom downstairs — he would have seen that there was a gleam in her eyes and a look of determination upon her face that, taken together, would have caused Miss Bascom the utmost uneasiness. Young Miss Liddiard, Miss Bascom had learned to her sorrow, was a strong believer in the active support of any cause, no matter how odd, that had enlisted her interest, and no amount of lecturing or persuasion had ever been able to convince her that young ladies should leave such matters to their elders — or, better still, to the Authorities, if it was a question of homeless cats or abused horses, as it had been upon two memorable occasions in Queen Square.

CHAPTER

2

The simultaneous arrival of Trimmer with the hartshorn and of a fatherly looking, grey-haired surgeon put a halt, however, to any immediate plans Eugenia had to delve further into the life history of her new-found cousin. She was banished to her own bedchamber while Dr. McCarey examined his patient; but she left the door slightly ajar as she changed from her travelling-dress and brushed her hair, and when she heard the doctor come out into the passage again she emerged to intercept him before he could reach the stairs.

"Did he pay you?" she enquired, coming to the point at once. The doctor's busy grey brows rose in some surprise. "Did he pay you your fee?" Eugenia repeated patiently. "I don't suppose he has much money, and after all I was the one who had you called, so I think it is only fair if I pay for it."

She began to open her reticule, but the doctor, with an air of slight amusement, assured her that his patient had already taken care of the matter.

"A relation of yours, Miss —?"

"Liddiard," supplied Eugenia readily. "Yes, he is my cousin. Is he very ill?"

Dr. McCarey said bluntly that as far as he had been able to ascertain his patient had the constitution of an ox, but that even an ox, if it had been sitting on the roof of a coach in pouring rain for half a dozen hours when it was just recovering from a fever, might experience some difficulty in navigating when it got down.

"A few weeks of rest and quiet living and he'll be right as a trivet," he said. "Any more of this skip-brained sort of behaviour, though, and I won't rule out inflammation of the lungs. Do his people live near here? You'd best get word to

31

them to look after him. You're not travelling with him yourself, I understand?"

"No," said Eugenia. "But I'll see that he's looked after. Thank you very much."

"A bowl of hot chicken broth and some arrowroot jelly," the doctor recommended. "And see that he doesn't stir out of the house again until this downpour ends," and he turned again towards the stairs.

Eugenia said good-bye to him, stood thoughtfully for a few moments in the passage, and then walked to the door of Richard Liddiard's bedchamber and scratched purposefully upon it.

"Come in," said the pleasant, lazy voice, so like her cousin Gerald's, but with a deeper note in it than Gerald's had ever had. But perhaps, she thought, Gerald's voice would be different now, too, less boyish than when she had last heard it. He would, after all, be as old now as this young man looked to be, somewhere in his middle twenties.

She opened the door and walked into the room.

Richard Liddiard was lying upon the bed as she had left him, but he sat up upon her entrance.

"No, don't get up," she said, coming over and standing beside the bed. "I only came to tell you that I've talked to that doctor, and he says you are to have chicken broth and arrowroot jelly for your supper, and then you must rest and be quiet for a few weeks. Can you do that?" She eyed rather doubtfully the shabby olive-green coat, which lay on a chair beside the bed. "You don't look very prosperous," she said.

He looked at her, an amused smile lighting his face for the first time since she had met him.

"You don't believe in beating about the bush, do you?" he asked.

"No. It never does much good, does it? I mean, it seems a bit idiotish trying to be tactful if there is something you really want to know."

"And what do you want to know about me, Miss Liddiard?"

"You may call me Eugenia, if you like. After all, we *are* cousins — not very close ones, but I always called Gerry Gerry, and he is related to me in the same way that you are. His father was Papa's cousin, too, you know." She put the coat on the bed and sat down on the chair where it had lain. "What I want to know," she said, "is whether you have anyone who will look after you until you're in plump currant again. You're not married, are you?"

"No."

"I thought not. You haven't a married look. And you can't have any brothers or sisters if both your parents died when you were born. But there might be someone else — Have you friends in England?"

"No. I haven't been in England for ten years. The only friend I have left here is a Yorkshireman named Ned Trice who became a jockey, went to the bad, and now keeps a very disreputable tavern in Tothill Fields. Look here, Miss Eugenia Liddiard, this is not in any possible way your affair —"

"Well, it wouldn't be, if I could find anyone else that it *was* their affair," Eugenia said reasonably, if not very grammatically. "But I can't just walk off and let you die of inflammation of the lungs or something ghastly like that."

"I have no intention of having inflammation of the lungs. *Or* of dying of anything whatever, if that's of any comfort to you."

"Yes, but I daresay you hadn't any intention of swooning away in the coffeeroom downstairs just now, either, but you did," Eugenia pointed out. "I hate being ill, too, but I had scarlet fever when I was twelve and I was disgustingly weak for almost a month afterwards." She looked at him critically. "I don't think you are fit for any sort of work just now," she said. "You *are* obliged to work at something, I expect?"

"Yes. I'm on my way to Newton Chase, Sir Harry Pyatt's place in Oxfordshire. He's in need of someone to manage his stables, I understand."

Eugenia regarded him with increased interest. "Oh, are you good with horses?" she asked. "Papa had a small stud at Coverts — that was our place in Kent — but when my cousin Cedric inherited it he sold all the horses off. He is in orders, you see, and lives in Canterbury." A sudden thought struck her. "Do you know," she said, "if you really are Cousin Charles's son — I mean his *real* son, legally and all that — Coverts should rightfully belong to you. Because Cousin Charles was Cousin Cedric's *elder* brother, you see, and so *he* would have been the heir if he had lived, and of course his son, if he was dead himself —"

"It sounds rather complicated," the young man said uninterestedly. "And at any rate there's not much point in thinking of that now, is there?"

"There would be," said Eugenia, who did not give up easily, "if you could prove —"

"Well, I can't," Richard Liddiard said dampingly. "That marriage took place a quarter of a century ago, and the clergyman who raised me made every possible enquiry, not twelve months afterwards, without the least success."

Eugenia said that in her opinion clergymen were not very enterprising, but, seeing that her companion, who had not obeyed her injunction to lie down again, was looking very tired, she forbore to press the matter and returned instead to the problem of his immediate future.

"If I were you," she said to him, "I shouldn't go to Newton Chase. I've met Sir Harry, and he is a horrid man. Papa said he tried to bribe Frank Buckle to lose a race at Newmarket, though of course it was never proved. And he has new grooms and trainers in every week, because he flies into a pelter and dismisses the old ones, and he has put down his stables twice. I shouldn't wonder if he were to do it again." She saw that one black brow was cocked at her disbelievingly. "No, truly!" she protested.

"Not pitching me a Banbury tale to keep me playing the invalid here?"

"Oh, no. I hardly ever tell lies," Eugenia said seriously. "I'm not a very good liar, you see. Besides, it would be a rather shabby thing to do, wouldn't it? — because I daresay you *do* need the work."

"I do," Richard assured her. "And, what is more, having no other present prospects than Sir Harry, I shall have to make do with trying my luck with him."

Eugenia wrinkled her brows. "It was a rather chancy thing to do, wasn't it?" she asked. "Coming all the way from Ireland just on the strength of a tip. Did you get it from your friend Ned Trice?"

"The answer is yes, and I daresay it was," said the young man equably. "But then, you see, I'm used to taking chances. That's how I went to Ireland in the first place."

"Did you run away?"

"Oh, no. Not really. I had nothing to run away from."

"The clergyman died?" she hazarded.

"Yes. His sister had some idea of apprenticing me to an apothecary as the best way to get me off her hands, but I rather thought not. So I went to Ireland instead."

Eugenia sighed enviously. "It sounds lovely," she said. "If I had been a boy, I'd have gone off on my own, too, when Papa died. Then I shouldn't have been obliged to go to that *odious* school, or live at Mere." She got up. "But that's neither here nor there," she said decisively. "You looked fagged to death, and I oughtn't to be keeping you talking to me. I'll order your supper and then after you've had it you can go to sleep." At the doorway she paused. "I daresay you haven't enough money to stop here for a few weeks?" she asked, with her schoolboy's matter-of-factness.

"You must think me a very improvident sort of fellow," said Richard Liddiard, who was indeed, as she had observed, looking very tired, but still had a faint, amused smile for her bluntness. "A fortnight in a Bristol inn, with a surgeon's fee to boot, was a bit more than I had bargained for, you see —"

"And I haven't so much as sixpence left from my quarter's allowance to lend you; I bought presents for all those stupid girls when I left Miss Bascom's," Eugenia said regretfully. "Oh, well! I daresay I shall think of something."

And she went off to find the landlord and order Richard Liddiard's supper, after which she sat down, in the pink parlour adjoining her own bedchamber, to a very good meal of Hessian soup, a boiled

39

duck with onion sauce, and a dish of salsify fried in butter, topped off by some fresh-baked Queen cakes.

It was while she was nibbling the Queen cakes that the idea came to her. It was an idea of such brilliant simplicity that she wondered she had not thought of it before, and she was on her feet and halfway to the door under the impetus of her desire to communicate it immediately to Richard Liddiard when she brought herself up short, recollecting the doctor's injunction for rest and quiet for his patient. Perhaps, she thought reluctantly, it would be best to wait until morning. He would be bound to have to think the idea over, to consider it in the tiresome way in which most people seemed to deal with the opportunities with which life presented them, and he really ought to go off to sleep at once instead.

So she sat for half an hour at the parlour window, which overlooked the courtyard and offered a very satisfactory view through its streaming panes, seriatim, of the arrival of a smart mail-coach, splashing up to the door to the discomfiture of a thin gentleman in gaiters just alighting from a post-chaise; the exertions of a pair of ostlers in plush waistcoats and corduroy breeches as they figged out a fresh team and put them to the mail-coach with a celerity born of their desire to get in out of the wet as soon as possible; and a spirited altercation between a farmer and a carrier over a brace of ducks that were apparently to be sent on to the next village. The coach-lanterns cast their wavering, dancing lights over this animated scene, catching the driving silver rods of the rain as they hissed down upon the dark cobblestones, and Eugenia, when Trimmer reminded her that they must be early on the road tomorrow, with a strong hint that she, at least, was longing for her bed, turned back reluctantly into the snug, candle-lit parlour.

As she lay in her bed a little later, with the rain still drumming relentlessly against the windowpanes, she perfected her plans for the morrow. Not that they needed a great deal of consideration, the main difficulty, it appeared to her, lying in the necessity of convincing Richard Liddiard that her solution to his present dilemma was one that he could properly accept. If he really were Gerry, she thought, instead of being only his double, there would be no difficulty at all; Gerry would have seen the whole thing as a great lark, and would have entered into it with all imaginable gusto.

But she could not help feeling that Richard Liddiard was a far different sort of person. Older, of course, than the Gerry she had known, but different in other ways as well — more aloof, more self-contained, with a vein of hard, cool determination quite unlike Gerry's quicksilver volatility.

In the midst of her reflections she drifted off to sleep.

When she awoke, Trimmer was running back the curtains of her bed and opening the blinds to reveal the pale light of a rather watery-looking but definitely fair morning. She had, she said, already been downstairs to enquire of the landlord as to the state of the roads, and had been told that there had been a washout between

Thatcham and Reading; but it was expected that by midmorning they might expect to find travel safe enough for their chaise.

"Good!" said Eugenia, and jumping out of bed, she made a hasty toilette, ordered a substantial breakfast, and went off to see Richard Liddiard.

She found him in his room in shirt and breeches, shaving, and looking remarkably unwelcoming as she made it clear to him that she expected to be invited inside.

"Where," he demanded, "is that abigail of yours? Doesn't she take the slightest care to see to it that you don't go haring off to strange men's bedchambers before breakfast?"

"Trimmer? She's really not a bad sort, when you get to know her," Eugenia said tolerantly. "I say, I've had the most brilliant idea, but I can't tell you about it standing out here in the passage."

"Then you can wait and tell me about it in the coffeeroom."

"No, I can't tell you there, either. Someone would be sure to overhear. I'll tell you what, if you really are going to be stuffy about it, you can come to my private parlour as soon as you finish shaving. You can't have any objection to that. But you don't look fit to be up yet," she added as a parting shot, as she backed off down the corridor towards her own rooms again.

A minute later she was wondering if she had done the right thing to leave him so readily. He might, she thought, simply walk downstairs and go off on one of the coaches or carriers that were already rattling into the courtyard, their wheels and bodies thickly splashed with mud after their hard triumph over the miry roads. He looked the independent sort.

But the knock that fell on the door a few minutes later brought not only a waiter bearing a well-laden tray but Richard Liddiard as well, shaven and pale, and still looking very impervious to persuasion.

"Come in and have some breakfast," Eugenia said hospitably. "At least, I daresay you ought still to be having arrowroot jelly or something horrid of

44

that sort, but I expect toast and coffee won't hurt you."

"Thank you," said Richard, "but I'll have breakfast in the coffeeroom."

"Oh, very well," she said, quite unruffled by this rebuff. "But you can come in for a minute, at any rate. There is something I *must* say to you," she added, as the waiter departed.

Richard Liddiard, apparently reassured by the presence of Trimmer in the background, came in; but he had reckoned without Eugenia's resourcefulness. There was, she said, lifting the covers of the dishes upon the tray, no ham, and she particularly remembered instructing Trimmer to order ham. A nice crozzly piece, fried to a turn, and would Trimmer please go downstairs and see to it? Trimmer, with a disapproving primming of her lips, went off after a moment's hesitation, and Eugenia at once turned to her guest.

"We haven't much time so I'll have to tell you quickly," she said, with a serious air. "I have been thinking, and it seems to me that the best thing you can do will be to pretend you are my cousin Gerry and come back to Mere with me for a few weeks, until you are in better frame. No one will know the difference; in fact, there soon won't even be any of the family at Mere, because Gussie — Lady Chandross — is taking me up to London for the Season almost at once, and Cecil is there — I mean in London — already. And I can find out from Haggart — he was our stud groom at Coverts, and Cecil took him on at Mere when Papa died — whether there is any sort of place open that will suit you when you are up to doing a job. Haggart has worked in racing stables for forty years, and he knows everyone on the turf —"

She broke off, looking doubtfully at Richard Liddiard, who had taken a deep breath and appeared about to embark upon just the sort of reply she had been afraid of.

"I do think you ought to consider it before you say no," she said hastily. "After all, *I* didn't know you weren't Gerry, and if I didn't, it isn't likely anyone at Mere will, either. You see, I knew him better than any of them — he was always away from Mere at school or at Oxford, and he spent all his holidays with Papa and me at Coverts. And no one at Mere has seen him at all for three years. As for coaching you about all the things you ought to know — of course Trimmer will be in the chaise with us, but she is not very quick, and if I talk to you all the way to Mere about the people there you should be able to gather enough information to see you through, without her being any the wiser about what we are up to. And if you *do* get into a sticky spot," she went on even more hastily, seeing the unencouraging expression upon Richard Liddiard's face, "you can always do what Gerry would do himself — turn sulky and say nothing at all, or simply pretend you were joking, the way I thought you were doing when you didn't recognise me last evening."

She paused once more. The distinctly skeptical expression had not left Richard's face.

"I see," he said politely. "You've thought it all out. And if Mr. Gerald

Liddiard himself turns up while I am carrying on this masquerade —?''

''Well, I *don't* think it is at all likely that he will,'' said Eugenia. ''After all, he hasn't done it for three years; it's much simpler, you see, just to write.''

''If even a letter arrived while I was in the house, I should very definitely be lurched, you know.''

''Yes, I've thought of that, but after all one has to take *some* risks. And it's not very likely that he *will* write just now; it's too soon after the Cheltenham affair. He tried to run off to Gretna with the daughter of a rich ironmonger, you see, and it cost Cecil a really appalling amount of money to get him out of *that* scrape.''

''I see.'' There was a wry twist to Richard Liddiard's mouth. ''Not an entirely scrupulous sort of fellow, your cousin Gerald.''

''I've told you he isn't.'' Eugenia looked at him, raising her chin. ''But it really is *quite* a good idea,'' she said, ''and will solve all your problems splendidly, though you don't seem to think so.''

"How do you know that I don't think so?"

"By the way you look. People always look at you like that when they think you have windmills in your head. Mostly it's because they've no imagination. You had better sit down, hadn't you?" she added, after a moment. "You're still horridly weak, I expect. Are you sure you won't have breakfast, after all? They've sent up lashings."

Richard said no, he would not have breakfast, and propped his shoulders against the doorframe in lieu of sitting down.

"So you won't do it?" Eugenia said, much disappointed.

"I haven't said so." She glanced up at him, surprised, and saw an odd, considering, cynical expression in his heavy-lidded dark eyes. "As a matter of fact," he said deliberately, "you are offering me the opportunity to do something I have wished to do for a long time — make the acquaintance of my noble relations —"

"Well, there isn't anyone at Mere just

now who is actually your *relation* except Gussie, and she is only by marriage," Eugenia pointed out. "Oh, and the children, of course, but they are still in the nursery. I've told you Cecil is in London, and I don't know why he should return before you will be fit to leave. If he did, he would give you a frightful bear-jaw, because he would think you were Gerry, naturally, and he and Gerry never did get on."

"Then why should you think that he — or Lady Chandross — will welcome me to Mere Court?"

"Oh, they won't exactly *welcome* you," Eugenia acknowledged. "But they'll *have* you. After all, Gerry *is* family. And in a place as big as Mere — there are ninety rooms, you see, and dozens and dozens of servants, besides Cecil's secretary and his chaplain and his steward, and heaven knows how many other people that Gussie always has cluttering around — one person more or less doesn't make a great deal of difference. But they *will* look after you there until you're well, which is the important thing, it seems to me. And as far as your losing the chance of having Sir Harry Pyatt take you on if you go to Mere," she added, "I should think you might very well have lost it already by being ill for a fortnight in Bristol, to say nothing of his *not* being the sort of person you would care to be employed by in the first place." Richard said nothing, and she looked at him enquiringly. "I'm right — aren't I?" she demanded.

"Yes," he said. "You are." The odd, detached, considering look was still there on his face, and after a moment he said decisively, to her great surprise, "Very well. I daresay I shall be able to brace it through. I'm on."

"You mean you really will do it? I didn't think you would. I thought you'd be too —"

"Honest? My dear Miss Liddiard, I have been living by my wits since I was fifteen, and poverty doesn't breed scruples. And, at any rate, this is an opportunity not many people are given — to step into the life they might have led except for the accident of a single missing scrap of paper. I should never forgive myself if I didn't grasp it."

She was still looking at him in slight puzzlement when the door opened and Trimmer came in again.

"They will bring the ham up in just a moment, dear Miss Liddiard," Trimmer said, and looked rather nervously at Richard.

Eugenia gathered her wits together. "Trimmer," she said, in her most matter-of-fact voice, "my cousin Gerald is returning to Mere with me. Will you see that his portmanteau is put into the chaise?" She turned to Richard. "And now, Gerry," she said, "shall we sit down to breakfast?"

"By all means," said Richard Liddiard.

CHAPTER

3

The chaise was able to set out before ten, and made such good progress, in spite of the initially very miry roads, that by early afternoon they were in London and by five had arrived at Mere Court. Eugenia, who had improved the hours by chattering away indefatigably about past and present family history except when she saw Richard looking so grey with fatigue that she stopped talking and allowed him to doze off against the claret-velvet cushions of the elegantly comfortable chaise, had known Mere since her childhood; she was therefore quite unimpressed when they turned in at the Gate House, with the Chandross coat of arms emblazoned over its broad stone archway, and entered the long avenue leading to the house, which was built in the form of a great central block crowned from behind by a high dome and flanked by one-storey wings that broke forward to contain a terraced forecourt.

But she saw the sudden alertness that overcame her companion's weariness when his eyes fell upon it, and he took in to the full its grandiose magnificence. The house had been an extravagance of the second Earl of Chandross, who had flourished a hundred years before and whose architect, bent upon out-Vanbrughing Vanbrugh, had produced a Baroque showplace that had been cursed by all his descendants since, saddled as they were with the task of maintaining its monumental splendour. In style it was a daring mixture of periods — Roman, mediaeval, and Tudor — and in size it rivalled Blenheim.

Eugenia, fearing that Richard's mask of familiarity, maintained with admirable poise during the journey, might momentarily be forgotten in his interest in what he saw, said to him meaningly as the chaise bowled on up the long, straight drive, "It's nice to be home again — isn't it?"

"Home?" he turned to look at her, his eyes blank for a single instant. Then the mask returned. "Oh — yes. It is."

Probably, it occurred to her, he had not expected quite so much magnificence; and she recalled her own childhood amazement at the sheer bulk of that grand façade when she had first been taken to visit here, and her conviction, when she had followed the footmen bearing their portmanteaux along the dramatic tunnel of the corridor that ran right through the centre of the house and both wings, that they had walked for miles before they reached the bedchambers that had been assigned to them.

But Richard Liddiard, reared in that most austere and correct of environments, a country parsonage inhabited by a scholarly incumbent, and exposed in later years to the ruder but more affluent elegancies of life among the

Irish squirearchy, was not, she saw, going to let Mere Court throw him off his balance. When he walked in at the front door beside her and surrendered his hat to Gleaves, the butler, his eyes flickered over the giant proportions of the two-storeyed stone hall, its monumental chimney piece of Sicilian pink and white marble, and its attendant gallery of marble statues, as if he had known them all his life.

The butler, who was new — the servants at Mere always were new, as Lord Chandross had a peevish temper and Lady Chandross a very volatile one — looked enquiringly at him as he greeted Miss Liddiard and consigned her chip-hat and duffle-cloak into the hands of a waiting footman.

"Oh — Gleaves," said Eugenia carelessly, "this is my cousin, Mr. Gerald Liddiard. I've brought him home with me for a short visit. I expect Lady Chandross will wish to have a bedchamber made ready for him. Where *is* Lady Chandross? Is she engaged?"

Gleaves said he believed her ladyship

was in her dressing room at the moment.

"Thank you; we'll go up," said Eugenia at once, and, turning to Richard, she added sedately, "Come along, Gerry." As they walked off together she continued, *sotto voce*, "Call her Gussie, and if she looks as if she would like to be kissed, do. She is fond of *galanterie* and frightfully fashionable, and she rather likes Gerry; he's her sort. I'll tell her you've been ill and about your collapsing at the King's Head, so you needn't come to dinner or see her again today. If she asks — you went to Ireland after that Cheltenham affair I spoke to you about on the journey, and you can tell her anything you like about what has happened after that."

She was pleased to see that Richard was regarding her with no evidence of apprehension on his dark face as they mounted one of the twin branches of the great curving staircase that led to the upper floor. He was managing, in fact, to look quite indifferent to the grandeur of his surroundings, which, she thought with respect, was a considerable achievement, particularly in his present state of health.

57

He, for his own part, appeared to be properly appreciative of the aplomb with which she had carried off the situation below.

"I thought," he remarked, as she led him down the long, first-floor corridor towards Lady Chandross's apartments, "you told me you were a very poor liar."

"Oh, this isn't *lying* — it's *acting*," she assured him. "And, after all, it's in a very good cause."

"And if I'm found out —? What will they do to you in that case?"

"Do to me?" She stared at him in astonishment. "Oh," she said, after a moment, "I see what you mean — will they do something horrid? You needn't trouble yourself over *that*. Gussie will probably say it is too, too dreary of me to have taken up with such an unsuitable young man, and she knows I'll find Lord This or Sir That much more amusing when we go up to London. And no one will tell Cecil about it at all because he has dyspepsia when he's upset and, besides, he has much more important things to think of."

Richard looked down at her. "In other words, no one will care a rush about you."

She lifted a thin shoulder. "Actually," she said, with an air that he felt must be a very young imitation of the cool ennui she had indicated would be Lady Chandross's reaction to her discovery of the truth of the situation, "it saves a great deal of trouble. Didn't *you* find it so when you were left alone in the world?" — and Richard Liddiard, who had for ten years pushed into the back of his mind the memory of the fifteen-year-old boy who had set his face for Ireland in the sure knowledge that his disappearance not only from England but even from the face of the earth would cause no emotion but relief in the breasts of those whose charge he had become, took the time, even at this chancy moment, to make a mental resolve that young Miss Eugenia Liddiard would never suffer from the consequences of the concern she had shown for him, if he was able to prevent it.

She had led him to one of the tall, pedimented doors that punctuated the long corridor, and now, with a conspiratorial glance at him, scratched upon it and was bidden to enter by a bored, rather husky feminine voice. Eugenia opened the door and Richard walked in behind her. He was, he saw, in an elegant boudoir hung with rose-pink brocade, with a glimpse through an open doorway into an adjoining bedchamber, the chief item of its furnishings — a tent-bed with its blue and silver draperies upheld by Cupids — overspread with a number of bandboxes, from which silver paper and several extremely fashionable bonnets were spilled out upon the blue silk coverlet.

The slender, handsome, thirtyish lady who sat regarding herself in the dressing-table mirror also wore a fashionable bonnet upon her fair hair — a daring celestial-blue creation with a jockey-front, trimmed with a forest of curling plumes.

"Oh, here you are at last, my dear!" she said, catching sight of Eugenia in the mirror in which she was critically regarding her own reflection. "Whatever has made you so late? Do you like this bonnet? I had Fanchon send down half a dozen from London, but I'm not *quite* sure — Gerry!" she broke off suddenly, as she became aware of the presence of a second visitor. She turned about in her chair to face Richard Liddiard, an incredulous smile curving her lips. "Gerry, you rogue! It *is* you! Where in heaven's name have *you* sprung from?"

"I ran across him quite by accident at the King's Head in Thatcham," Eugenia said, flinging herself hastily into the breach. "We were obliged to lie there instead of at Speenhamland because of the state of the roads. And he has been horridly ill, and hasn't a feather to fly with, so I thought you wouldn't mind if I brought him back with me to Mere —"

"Mind? I'm delighted! We are desperately dull here just now. Cecil has gone to London; Robin and Vinnie Carstairs have been called to Scotland because his aunt is dying — yes, *again,* my dears — and I am left with absolutely no one in the house but the Beaminsters, and you *know* how frightfully uninteresting *they* are." Lady Chandross presented a thin, rouged cheek to Richard, who kissed it, Eugenia saw admiringly, with composure and, taking the bejewelled hand she offered to him, held it audaciously for a few moments longer than mere civility required.

"No, you wicked boy, you haven't changed! Give me back my hand," Lady Chandross said, looking quite well-pleased in a bored sort of way. "But, my dear, that *dreary* coat!" she went on, her eyebrows going up as she surveyed the offending garment. "You must certainly be all to pieces to put anything so shabby on your back! Where have you been? You haven't found another heiress to run off with — that goes without saying!"

"No," he said, in his deep, lazy voice. "I've been in Ireland. It's horses, not women, one looks for there, you know."

"If I know you, you have been looking for both — and have found no luck in either direction," Lady Chandross said. "You must tell me all about it —"

"Not now," Eugenia said firmly. "He has been ill, Gussie — I had to call a surgeon to him at the King's Head, because he fainted dead away in the coffeeroom, and he said he was to have complete rest and quiet for a few weeks. That's why I brought him here. And he has been jolted about over those horrid roads all day —"

Lady Chandross surveyed Richard Liddiard's face, which was certainly extremely pale under its bronze.

"Yes, you *do* look burnt to the socket," she said. "My dear, how *dreary* for you! *And* for me — just when I was thinking you had been sent from heaven to make dinner not *quite* insupportable this evening. Broaddis!" she called, and the smart abigail who had been returning the bonnets upon the bed to the bandboxes came into the room. "Tell Mrs. Hopkins the Blue Bedchamber for Mr. Gerald, and he will be dining there this evening. I daresay broth and syllabub and those dreary invalidish sort of things; tell her he has been ill. Cecil would fly into a dreadful pelter if he saw you in this house," she went on without pause to Richard, as Broaddis left the room. "He said he would see you in the Fleet before he towed you out of the River Tick again, after you had cost him that monstrous sum over that affair of the brewer's daughter —"

"Ironmonger's daughter," Richard corrected her scrupulously, with a glance at Eugenia.

"Well, I'm sure it doesn't signify whether the creature's father was an ironmonger or a brewer; I only know he bled poor Cecil dreadfully," Lady Chandross said, going back once more to a contemplation of her reflection in the mirror. "Do you like this bonnet, Gerry darling? I shall rely on your word; you always have had charming taste."

Richard said promptly that he found it the acme of à la modality, and was then at once borne off by Eugenia, who said with a feeling of relieved exhilaration as the door closed behind them, "Well! I must say you carried that off splendidly! How did you know Gerry would have held her hand like that?"

"You've given me a fair idea of the sort of character I'm supposed to have," said Richard. He was showing his own reaction to his successful imposture only by a slight air of added alertness, which failed, however, to destroy the general appearance of cool composure that Eugenia had noted in his manner from the start of their acquaintance. "It's not an uncommon type, you know."

"But not your type?" She gave him an enquiring glance as they walked along the corridor together.

"No."

"I'm glad." She smiled at him suddenly. "Gerry was frightfully silly about women," she confided. "But they seemed to like it. *I* shouldn't. Compliments and such flummery." She indicated a door to their right. "That's my room. And the Blue Bedchamber is just down the hall. That will be convenient if you should need to consult me. And, by the way — Mrs. Hopkins is the housekeeper; she has been here less than a year, so she'll never have seen Gerry. The only one of the servants you really need worry about is Haggart, and if *he* discovers you are not Gerry I can take care of that. He is very shrewd, but he's also my best friend here at Mere."

She saw him safely bestowed in the Blue Bedchamber, where a footman was just bringing in his unimpressive portmanteau while a housemaid, already despatched by Mrs. Hopkins, came hurrying in with towels and hot water, and went back to her own room to find Trimmer unpacking her belongings and laying out a demure white muslin evening frock for her. Now that she was about to make her come-out, she had been given to understand that she was to take her meals in the great dining room with the Chandrosses and their guests, instead of being relegated to the nursery with their two small sons and the governess, where she had previously dined when she was at Mere. The thought was not agreeable, for she disliked the ceremony that invested the rite of dinner at Mere Court, where even when the covers were not enlarged for guests the family ate in oppressive splendour, attended by a small army of servants in claret-and-silver livery and seated upon chairs upholstered in green Genoese velvet set about a long table centred beneath a large Baroque illusionist ceiling-painting counterfeiting the interior of a dome and surrounded by putti and allegorical female figures in high relief.

But she told herself with some severity that if Richard Liddiard could carry off his role as Gerald in a house and with a set of people he had never seen before, she herself should be able to take a very inconspicuous part in the ceremony of dinner at Mere Court without making a piece of work over it. She knew quite well, at any rate, that no one would pay her the least attention, except perhaps for Lord Chandross's chaplain, Mr. Mortimore, who was a youngish man and a bachelor and had begun to embarrass her recently by gazing upon her rather more persistently than she felt mere civility demanded and discoursing to her at tedious length concerning the commentary he was engaged in writing on one of the minor prophets.

But Mr. Mortimore, she saw with some relief when she entered the Long Gallery where the family and their guests customarily foregathered before dinner, had been seized upon by the Beaminsters, mother and daughter, who were ardent readers of sermons and other theological works and, being ladies of great energy and inflexible self-confidence, were bent upon teaching him his business. Eugenia, on the other hand, was surprised to find herself taken up for once by Lady Chandross, who wanted to hear all about her meeting with the supposed Gerald Liddiard. This was soon told, as Eugenia was not anxious to add any details to the story she had already given.

"And he didn't tell you what he was doing in this part of the country?" Lady Chandross asked, when she had finished.

"No. Oh — only something about finding work —"

"Work? Gerry?" Lady Chandross lifted her thin shoulders incredulously. "My dear child, how too naïve of you to believe that! Ten to one it is a woman — or a horse — or a wager. I do hope, though, that he isn't planning an extended stay here; Cecil will fly up into the boughs at the mere mention of such a thing. In fact, Gerry is showing far more courage than I should have given him credit for to turn up here at all, after what has gone on over the past several years. But he *has* changed a good deal — don't you think? Older, of course, but — more serious, too? Where in heaven's name," she continued without a change of tone, as her eyes went over Eugenia's muslin gown, "*did* you get that dreadful frock?"

"Miss Bascom bought it for me. She said you wrote her I was to have something suitable."

"Suitable! Heavens!" Lady Chandross shuddered. "I see I shall have to send you to Fanchon the moment we arrive in town. No man of fashion will pay you the slightest degree of attention if you appear at Almack's in a frock so completely out of the fashion."

"I don't expect," Eugenia said frankly, "that they will look at me anyway. I'm not the proper type."

But Lady Chandross, who had not the least notion of being burdened with the task of chaperoning a young girl about for more than the absolute minimum of time required to get her off into some sort of

69

eligible marriage, would have none of this.

"Nonsense!" she said. "You are dark — which is fortunate, for blondes are not at all in fashion this year — and you have a lovely figure: one must give you that. With the right clothes, you may 'take' very well. There is a young man who is the son of a friend of Cecil's, Sir William Walford — a younger son and Sir William's fortune is merely a comfortable one, so there is very little to be expected from *that* direction; but young Walford himself has a promising career before him in the political field, Cecil thinks: *he* might do very well for you. And there is Lord Cazden's youngest; he is in the diplomatic service and Sir Charles Stuart *may* do something for him there — there is a vague family connexion. Of course we can't hope for anything in the way of fortune or title, since you have none of your own to offer, but if you will take the trouble to make yourself agreeable you will certainly be able to form a very eligible connexion, after all."

It was on the tip of Eugenia's tongue to

say that she was going to marry Tom Rowntree — whose existence, incidentally, she had all but forgotten in the rush of events since her departure from Miss Bascom's Select Academy; but prudence won the day. It would be better, she thought, to wait until she had had the opportunity to talk to Tom, or at least to hear from Muffet that he was agreeable to the plan they had concocted for his future, before she acquainted Gussie with the futility of her making lists of unknown young men who might be persuaded, in view of her cousin Cecil's powerful interest in the Government, to offer for her hand.

The arrival of Gleaves to announce that dinner was served interrupted the conversation at this point, and they all moved into the dining room, where she was able to enjoy almost undisturbed an excellent meal that began with a tureen of turtle and progressed through crimped salmon, turkey à la perigeux, cutlets of mutton braised with soubise sauce, and roast woodcock, to a charlotte of applies, a *gâteau mellifleur,* and several

71

creams and jellies.

Of these dishes she partook with an excellent appetite, but her mind was not upon them. She was thinking instead of Richard Liddiard, considering how one might go about proving the existence of a marriage that might, or might not, have been celebrated more than a quarter of a century before at a location that might range anywhere from Kent to the Continent.

Why she should feel it incumbent upon her to prove that marriage she could not precisely have said, but it had something to do, she thought, with a sense of belonging. She herself had been brought up "belonging" — Cecil might not care tuppence about her, but she knew that it would never have crossed his mind to reject her claim upon him as a Liddiard — and so she had a perhaps exaggerated view of the awfulness of being Richard Liddiard and belonging nowhere, of being obliged to assume another man's name and identity even to be allowed inside the front door of a house where he ought to have been welcomed without question, as she and Gerald were.

And then there was the thought of how much worse, how infinitely much worse, it would be if he ever saw Coverts. For to Eugenia, Coverts was not merely a good Kentish property, with a Tudor manor-house, so much altered and added to that it had lost any pretension to authentic style and now represented only a dwellingplace that people had lived in and loved over the centuries, standing as its centre. Coverts was, to her, the Liddiard belongingplace, the place where Liddiards had had their roots long before the Baroque magnificence of Mere Court had been thought of. And if Richard Liddiard was its rightful owner, nothing could be worse than seeing it and knowing that he would never be anything but a stranger to it.

Or at least it would be so if she were in Richard Liddiard's place. It might, she thought, not matter so much to him, just as it had never seemed to matter in that particular way to Cedric Liddiard, who, immersed in his own scholarly pursuits, considered Coverts and all its works as a burden, and one that, for family reasons, could not be cast upon the Lord. Nor had it mattered in that way to her cousin Gerald. But then Gerald had never cared a great deal about anything but having an amusing time.

And as she ate her *gâteau mellifleur,* she wondered for the first time where Gerald — the real Gerald — was now, and what would happen if, by some unlikely and malicious twist of fate, he were to turn up at Mere while Richard Liddiard was filling his shoes there.

CHAPTER

4

"Haggart," said Eugenia the next morning to Lord Chandross's head groom, "do you think it is ever right to deceive?"

Haggart give her a suspicious glance from under his craggy grey brows. He had just completed making the rounds of the stables with her, during the course of which she had renewed her acquaintance with all her favourites and had joined in his criticism of a washy bay — "a collection of bad points, and forever throwing out a splint," was Haggart's disparaging summation — recently purchased by Lord Chandross.

"What have you been up to?" he demanded after a moment, cannily reserving judgement.

"I can't tell you," said Eugenia, "unless you promise to keep it strictly confidential. You see, if Lord Chandross were to find out about it, he wouldn't like it above half."

Haggart spat, which might or might not have been an expression of his feelings concerning his employer. He had accepted Lord Chandross's offer of a position at Mere Court when Eugenia's father had died three years before, but his heart was still at Coverts, and only his settled opinion that Miss Eugenia needed someone to keep a rein upon her in that den of fools and iniquity she had fallen into had prevented him from consigning Lord Chandross and his distressingly mediocre stable of showy carriage-horses, hunters, and hacks to the devil long ago and finding more satisfactory employment with a gentleman who not only raced but knew a sound horse when he saw one.

"It's not likely I'd cry rope on you to *him,*" he said presently, after a companionable but, upon Eugenia's side, somewhat anxious silence during which he appeared to have been contemplating the matter. "What have you been deceiving him about?"

"It's not him exactly. At least not yet. And you haven't promised. You see, it's not *my* secret," she said hastily, as Haggart looked offended. "I'd trust you if it was only for myself. But there's someone else —"

"A man?" Haggart looked not only suspicious now but also incredulous. It was hard for him to believe that Miss Eugenia, whom he had set upon her first pony, was of an age when such a supposition was not only possible but natural; but a glance at the supple figure in its all but outgrown blue riding-dress confirmed the fact unmistakably. Haggart, putting two and two together and coming out with five, arrived at the conclusion that if there was deceiving going on, it was on the part of some black-hearted, lily-livered dandy, with Eugenia its unsuspecting intended victim, and said darkly, "You want to stay away from men, Miss Eugenia. Especially if it's deceiving they have in mind."

"But it wasn't his idea; it was mine," Eugenia explained. And, as Haggart still looked unforgiving, "Oh, very well," she said resignedly. "I expect I had best tell you about it from the beginning. You've heard, I daresay, that I brought my cousin Gerald back to Mere with me?"

Haggart had heard that Mr. Gerald was at Mere. That went without saying — at Mere, as in every other great house, the servants knew everything worth knowing about the family they served.

"Is it Mr. Gerald you're running some kind of rig for, then?" he said disapprovingly. "That shows little sense. He can get himself into the briars fast enough without any help from you."

"Yes, but it isn't Gerald I'm doing it for. You see, he isn't Gerald." Haggart stared. "I mean the man I brought back to Mere with me isn't Gerald," Eugenia went on to explain. "He is Charles Liddiard's son. You knew Charles Liddiard, didn't you, Haggart?"

They had reached the open stable door and Haggart's face, in the bright morning sunlight, showed no signs of astonishment, his code being that a man of his years and experience was immune to astonishment. But he sat down rather suddenly on the bench that stood outside the stable door.

"Mr. *Charles's* son?" he said.

"Yes." Eugenia recounted briefly the circumstances of her meeting with Richard Liddiard at the King's Head in Thatcham. "So you see I couldn't simply leave him there," she concluded, "ill and without a penny to bless himself with. And now he will need work, as soon as he is well enough for it, and I thought you might be able to help him with that —"

She broke off, seeing that Haggart was about to deliver himself of some pronouncement.

"Daft!" he said. "Clean daft, the pair of you."

"No, he's not in the least daft," Eugenia said seriously. "Wait until you meet him and you'll see. He looks amazingly like Gerry, but he's really not like him in the least. And he didn't want to come here, only I don't expect he quite knew what else to do."

"And if his lordship finds out? There'll be a rare dust kicked up then!" said Haggart. "He's the pattern of the old lord — you ken that well yourself — stiff-rumped, and a knaggy old gager when it comes to family! If this young chap is going about calling himself a Liddiard —"

"But he *is* a Liddiard — a real one, I mean," Eugenia insisted. "He says Charles Liddiard married his mother."

"Happen he did, happen he didn't," said Haggart, casting a malevolent eye upon a stable-boy who had been exercising one of Lord Chandross's hacks and was leading it into the stable to rub it down.

"Do *you* remember when it happened, Haggart? But you must. Do tell me all about it — please!"

Haggart said, grumbling, that he had better things to do than rake up old bits of scandal that had been forgotten for time out of mind — a preamble that in no wise discouraged Eugenia, for she knew that he liked nothing better than to tell tales of past Liddiard sins and glories. She composed herself on the bench beside him in the morning sunshine to listen, and bit by bit it all came out.

It was the usual story, it seemed, of a wild young man of good family and the pretty daughter of a neighbouring farmer. The Justises, the girl's family, were respectable people, Haggart said, and they had tried to keep Susan out of young Mr. Charles's way when they had seen how the wind was blowing. They had even sent her for a time to stay with an aunt in Yarmouth, but Mr. Charles had followed her there and made such a nuisance of himself that the aunt had packed her off home again in a huff. And the next thing anyone knew, the two of them had run off together.

No, not to Gretna; Lord Chandross — not the present one, but his old lordship, who had stood in the place of a father to Mr. Charles, Mr. Charles's own father being dead — had had them traced, and it was found they had gone to foreign parts. And no, Haggart had never heard any talk of a wedding, though he well remembered the storm that had blown up when, a year later, Susan Justis had written his lordship to say that Mr. Charles was dead and she had had a child by him, a boy.

"Signed it *Susan Liddiard,* she did," Haggart said, "and his lordship damning her up and down the house, the way I heard tell, to the scandal of all, and saying never a brass farthing would she get out of him for herself *or* her bastard unless she left off calling herself by a name she had no right to. And that was the last that was ever heard of her."

"Because she died then, too, you see," Eugenia said. "And so you think she really never was married —?"

"I didn't say that," Haggart said cautiously. Haggart was not one to commit himself unless he knew he was standing upon solid ground. "I don't know anything about it, one way or t'other. All I *do* know is, Mr. Charles had a rare coaxing tongue with the lasses; but then Susan Justis wasn't a light woman. Serious, she was, and the kind to keep herself to herself. I misdoubt she'd have gone off with any man without a wedding ring on her finger — though you can

82

never tell about wenches," he added disillusionedly. "Kittle-cattle they are, saying one thing and then doing another."

Eugenia was frowning over this piece of information.

"So if they *were* married, then, you think it might have been in Kent?" she said. "I mean, she wouldn't have gone off to the Continent with him merely on a promise? She wasn't that kind?"

"No, she wasn't that kind. A rare, quiet, prudent lass. But you can never tell —"

"Yes," said Eugenia, who was pursuing her own train of thought, "but if they *were* married, why shouldn't Charles Liddiard have written to tell his family about it? After all, he lived for almost a year after he and Susan Justis went off together."

"And have his lordship cut off his allowance for marrying beneath him and disgracing his name!" Haggart said. "Och, you didn't know Mr. Charles: that's plain! He was Mr. Gerald all over again — ready enough to get himself into a bumblebath, but not over keen to take the consequences. He knew the old lord wouldn't raise any dust over his having half a dozen light-o'-loves in keeping; but wedding a lass like Susan Justis all legal and proper — that 'ud be another matter! No, I don't think Mr. Charles would ha' been anxious to let his lordship know about *that*."

"And the Justises? Wouldn't they have known?" Eugenia persisted. "Perhaps Susan wrote to them —"

"Happen she did. But they were a close-mouthed set, all the Justises, and as much against Susan having aught to do with Mr. Charles as old Lord Chandross was himself. After she went off with him they never mentioned her name again, as far as ever I heard tell of it. Then the father died, and the mother and the two boys went off to America —"

"Oh, dear!" said Eugenia, much disappointed. "Are there none of them left now in Kent?"

Haggart said that to the best of his knowledge there were not, and, roused by the appearance in the stableyard of the coachman, with whom he had a mortal feud, and whom he darkly accused to

84

Eugenia of intentions of interfering with the bran poultice he had placed upon the foreleg of one of Lord Chandross's team of chestnuts, which had been badly grazed, owing solely, he averred, to the cowhandedness of the aforesaid coachman, got up and went off to join battle with him.

Eugenia herself went slowly and thoughtfully back to the house, and made her way to the Blue Bedchamber, where she found Richard Liddiard, unexpectedly resplendent in a brocade dressing gown, just completing a light breakfast.

"Good morning," she said. "How natty you are! You look ever so much better this morning."

Richard agreed that he felt very much better, and, indicating the gorgeous dressing gown with a grimace, said that Lady Chandross had looked in to see him for a moment, and, having taken exception to his own wardrobe, had despatched a servant to replenish it from Lord Chandross's.

"Thus completing my sensation of being in the predicament of the old lady with her petticoats cut off all around," he said — " 'Lack-a-mercy, this is none of me!' Look here, Miss Liddiard, I must get out of this, and at once. I must have been mad even to think of coming here."

"You weren't mad at all — only ill and I daresay at your wit's end," Eugenia said, sitting down and curling herself up comfortably opposite him in a bergère armchair.

"Don't do that!" Richard said sharply.

"Do what?"

"Sit down. You oughtn't to be here —"

"You really have very old-fashioned ideas, you know. After all, you *are* my cousin."

"I am Charles Liddiard's bastard," he said grimly, looking at her from under his heavy lids with an arrogance, she thought, that quite belied his words.

"*And* my cousin," she said, undaunted. "Besides, I don't believe you are — his bastard, that is. I have been telling Haggart about you —'

"*What!*"

"Well, I had to, if I want him to help you, so I decided to take him into my confidence. And it was a very good thing that I did," she added hastily, seeing from Richard's face that he was in no way pleased by her making so free of his true identity, "because he knows all about your mother's people — the Justises — and about your mother, too. And he says she wasn't the kind of girl who would have gone off with Charles Liddiard without a wedding ring. That means they must have been married in Kent, which will make matters much easier for us."

"For *us*?"

"Yes. You *did* come back to England — really, deep down, didn't you? — because you wanted to prove that marriage. I have been thinking about it, and it doesn't make sense any other way. I mean, you must know people in Ireland who would have been much more likely to give you a place than anyone here."

"You are," Richard assured her, but with a slight relaxation in the grimness of his manner, "a rather uncannily perceptive young woman, Miss Eugenia Liddiard. Very well — I do want to prove that marriage. But why you should make it a personal concern of yours —"

He broke off, seeing with surprise the sudden crimson that had risen in Eugenia's cheeks. She had been so totally unself-conscious up to this time of any oddity in her having placed herself upon terms of intimacy with a completely strange young man that this evidence of sudden embarrassment was, to say the least, astonishing.

And, in fact, it astonished Eugenia as well. Having been brought up almost exclusively in masculine company, in what had been, ever since her mother's death, a bachelor establishment at Coverts, she had managed to survive even Miss Bascom's obliquely warning homilies and the hothouse atmosphere of fashionable intrigue that pervaded Mere Court without a rift in the comfortable surface of her belief that men, young and old, were friendly creatures with whom sociable relations could readily be established. But it had suddenly occurred to her now, for no good reason that she could think of, that Richard Liddiard suspected that the interest she had displayed in his affairs had its basis more in the fact that she had conceived what Gussie and her set would have called a *tendre* for him than in altruistic motives; and it was this thought that had sent the blood into her cheeks.

She rose as abruptly as if she had been scalded.

"I shall have to go now," she said, with studied carelessness. "We are leaving for London in a very few days, and then you will have the house all to yourself, except for the servants, of course, so if I were you I shouldn't think of leaving just yet. It's quite safe; Haggart is as close as an oyster, and I'm sure he will know someone who can find a proper place for you when you're well enough for it."

Richard's air of surprise had vanished; he was looking at her with one black brow quizzically raised.

"Something I've said?" he enquired.

"What?" She looked at him with slight hauteur.

"Your sudden distaste for my company. I won't say I won't be relieved to have you leave this room, but if I've said or done the wrong thing I'd like to know. I'm really not such a clod, you know, as not to be grateful for what you've done for me."

"Oh — *that!*" Eugenia dismissed it, feeling happier. Perhaps he had not been thinking what she had feared, after all. "It's just that I didn't want you to think it was anything *personal,*" she confided, suddenly able to share her fear with him.

"Far be it from me," said Richard gravely, "to be such a coxcomb as to imagine anything of the sort."

"You see," said Eugenia, reassured, "I am probably going to marry Tom Rowntree very soon. The Rowntrees' land marches with ours — I mean what used to be ours," she corrected herself, "in Kent, and I've known him forever."

"My felicitations. But why *probably?*"

"Well, I haven't actually *asked* him yet."

"*You* haven't asked *him?*"

"Yes." Eugenia accepted with composure a question that would, Richard considered, have thrown any other young woman he had ever known into the greatest confusion. "I *do* think it is stupid for the man always to have to do the asking, don't you? I mean, it has probably never occurred to Tom what a very good idea it would be, simply because he hasn't had occasion to think of it. But we will both be obliged to marry *someone* some day — he is the Squire's only son, you see, and of course I don't wish to be hanging on Cecil's sleeve all my life — and we have always dealt famously with each other. So it should work out very well, don't you think?''

Richard said that, put in that way, he didn't see why it shouldn't, but added that Tom might not quite see it in that light.

''Oh? Why not?'' Eugenia looked surprised.

''Well — speaking only for myself, you understand — I think if I were in his shoes I'd prefer to do the asking myself. A stupid prejudice on my part, I expect — but there you are.''

''Oh yes, but Tom is different,'' Eugenia said confidently. ''We've known each other all our lives, you see, and he doesn't care any more than I do for that sort of romantic flummery.''

"Very sensible of him, I daresay; but if I were you, I'd still manage matters so that he is the one who does the asking."

She shrugged. "Well, I'll try," she conceded. "But I'm really not very good at that sort of thing. Gussie says I'm hopeless. I must say she is splendid at it herself. Cecil always does exactly what she wishes, only he thinks he's thought of it himself." She moved to the door. "She didn't suspect you weren't Gerry this morning, did she?" she asked.

"No. She stayed only for a moment. I gathered she had more important things on her mind than Gerald Liddiard."

"Oh, yes," said Eugenia tolerantly. "Lord Rushton. He is staying at the Towers and she expects him to ride over this morning. He's her latest."

"Her latest? I see. I may be — as you have said — remarkably old-fashioned, but it would appear to me that Lady Chandross is scarcely a suitable guardian for you."

"Oh, well. I don't see much of her when I'm at Mere," Eugenia said. "I spend a good deal more of my time with Haggart, and he is old-fashioned enough to satisfy even you. Shall I tell him you'll come to the stables and have a talk with him in a few days, when you're feeling in better frame?''

Richard hesitated for a moment. It was obvious to her what he was thinking — that he found his situation at Mere Court intolerable, an aberration into which he had been tempted only by the fatigue and confusion of his illness, and that he ought to cut himself free from it as soon as possible.

What was not obvious to her was the overwhelming pull towards remaining — even if only for a short time and under false pretences — as an accepted member of a family that had rejected him since the day he had been born. Here at Mere, even though he walked in another man's shoes, he was for the first time in his life a Liddiard, not some anonymous, chance-got bastard befriended by strangers and later cast upon the world by them.

Eugenia was watching the dark face, the unreadable dark eyes under the strongly marked black brows.

"You won't go before you do that — will you?" she asked rather anxiously. "Really, there's no reason why you shouldn't stay at least that long. You've seen for yourself that Gussie doesn't suspect, and there's no one else —"

Richard looked at her; a faint smile suddenly lit his eyes.

"Very well," he said. "You win. I shall stay. But I hope neither of us will have reason to regret it."

CHAPTER

5

It did not appear, as the late spring days passed and the oaks and beeches at Mere filled into heavier leaf, as wild rose and blackthorn, lady-smocks and campion, came into riotous bloom in the hedgerows, that either of them would have reason to regret it. Lady Chandross, absorbed in her own affairs, paid little heed to the manner in which Eugenia and the presumed Gerald Liddiard were filling their days. Eugenia might roam the countryside on the chestnut mare that was her particular favourite in Lord Chandross's stables; Richard might drowse in the Blue Bedchamber or rouse himself to walk down to the stables and discuss with

Haggart the shortcomings of the elegantly housed horses there, each with its own name over its box and a neatly plaited edging to its straw: she made few enquiries and seemed content to accept Richard's excuses for continuing to have his meals in the Blue Bedchamber instead of making a formal appearance in the dining room.

She told him once, frankly, that if he wished to avoid a thundering scold from Lord Chandross he would disappear before her husband had occasion to come to Mere again; but since Lord Chandross had every intention of doing the Season with her and she herself would be going up to London very shortly, there seemed no reason why his lordship should leave his rather pressing affairs in town for some time to come.

Meanwhile, Eugenia was delighted to see that Richard had, after an initial difficult half hour, been accepted by Haggart as a true Liddiard. On the first day that he had walked out to the stables with Eugenia, Haggart had regarded him with all the suspicion and dour reserve that he kept for one of Lord Chandross's new acquisitions; he was obviously prepared for the worst.

But as Eugenia, with Haggart grudgingly accompanying them, had taken him through the stables, as Haggart's own standoffishness had been met with that quiet, pleasant, impenetrable reserve that Eugenia had already learned to recognise as so characteristic of Richard Liddiard, Haggart's own reserve had perceptibly melted. And Richard knew horses. When he summed up in a glance a peacocky chestnut that was short of bone and ran a knowing hand over one of Chandross's hunters that was, to put it mildly, a little straight-shouldered, Haggart visibly relaxed.

"You'll be wanting to try one of these misbegotten creatures yourself when you're in better cue, I don't doubt, sir," he said; Eugenia noted that he avoided calling him "Mr. Gerald." "This is the best of them," and he led the way to where a bright sorrel with a high white stocking on one leg looked inquisitively out at them from his loose-box. "But no manners, and a rogue's temper, he has," Haggart continued. "The boys don't know how to handle him. Miss Eugenia's been at me to put a saddle on him for her; well, she has as good hands as any in England, but he's not a mount for a lady, as you can see for yourself."

Richard had said then that if Haggart would have a saddle put on the sorrel for him, he would be glad of the chance to take him out himself for half an hour, and though Haggart had looked doubtfully at the pallor beneath the bronze of the dark face and Eugenia had protested, this had been done. After that, Haggart's conquest had been complete. Mr. Gerald, he had confided to Eugenia later, wasn't a priming to this new-found Liddiard. A Liddiard like her own father, who would fling his leg across any piece of horseflesh that had ever been foaled and come home the master of it. He, Haggart, knew of more than one nobleman with a prestigious stud who would be happy to have such a man in his employ; but it was a pity, since this was indeed Mr. Charles's son, that he couldn't have Coverts and a stud of his own.

"Yes, but there is not the least use in our thinking of that unless we can prove somehow that Charles Liddiard really *did* marry Susan Justis," Eugenia said. "If we were in Kent we might at least make enquiries — there must be some record somewhere of that marriage if it really did take place — but there is no hope of doing that now, with everything in train for our leaving for London the day after tomorrow. I *had* thought of writing to Tom Rowntree and asking him to take the matter in hand, but I *don't* think he would be likely to make much of a fist of it."

With this Haggart thoroughly agreed. Master Tom, he said, was as sound a man after hounds as was his father, the Squire, which was saying a good deal, but if it was clever work that was wanted, they'd be coming to the wrong place.

"Well, I shall simply have to think of a scheme to get down to Kent myself soon," Eugenia said; which made Haggart regard her distrustfully, for Miss Eugenia's "schemes," as he was well aware, were more likely than not to end in her landing herself in the basket, even though they might be highly beneficial to the person she had been trying to help.

This conversation had taken place on the next to last day before Eugenia was to leave for London, and on the following day she and Richard had their last ride together, arguing amicably as they did so about Richard's determination to leave Mere on the following day as well and try his luck at obtaining a vacant post with Sir John Alloway in Leicestershire, which Haggart had heard of through an acquaintance of his. It was far enough from Mere, said Richard, that his resemblance to Gerald Liddiard would not be likely to arouse comment, and if he was well enough to roam Essex on horseback with Eugenia, he was well enough to do a job of work.

"An hour's easy hacking about in country lanes!" Eugenia said disparagingly. "But — oh well, I don't blame you for wanting to get away. I'm glad you've had this much time at Mere, though. At any rate, I don't think you'll go about collapsing in coffeerooms now."

She left him talking to Haggart and went up to the house, revolving in her mind the question of how, with herself in London and Richard in Leicestershire, enquiries about a marriage in Kent were to be satisfactorily pursued; but as she entered the hall on her way upstairs to her bedchamber she suddenly came upon a scene that surprised her to the extent that everything but what was going forward under her eyes flew instantly out of her head.

In the hall stood Lord Chandross, still in his driving-coat and evidently in a towering rage; before him a pair of anonymous-looking, half-cowed, but obviously determined men in blue coats and wide-brimmed hats; and beside him Lady Chandross, in a very fashionable morning-dress, but looking for once neither aloof nor bored.

"But, Cecil darling, of course it is all a stupid mistake!" she was expostulating, as Eugenia arrived upon the scene. "It can't possibly be Gerry they are looking for! Gerry is a scamp and a rogue — yes!

But an accusation like *this* —!"

"But you admit, madam — you admit he *is* staying in this house!" Lord Chandross gritted out, between clenched teeth.

"Yes, of course he is!" Lady Chandross looked slightly nervous, though she was brazening the matter out in good form, for when her husband, whose displeasure with her usually expressed itself only in the form of peevish remarks or disapproving silence, called her "madam" in that particular tone of voice she was well aware that trouble was in the wind. "I could hardly turn him out of doors when he was scarcely able to stand on his feet!" she defended herself volubly. "I made sure you wouldn't have wished me to do otherwise! And it is perfectly absurd to think that — whatever follies he may have fallen into — he is guilty of a thing like this! There *must* be some mistake. These men" — she turned her gaze venomously upon the two strangers, who looked more uncomfortable than ever, but stubbornly stood their ground — "these men have certainly made some monstrous error."

It was at that moment that Lord Chandross's eyes fell upon Eugenia, standing in the doorway with a stunned look upon her face, and encompassed Gleaves and a startled footman discreetly imitating in their demeanour a pair of the marble statues that ornamented the hall.

"Can't discuss the thing here!" he said testily to the two strangers, obviously wrestling for control over his temper. "Come along!"

He led the way into one of the small saloons that opened from the hall, and when they had entered slammed the door shut behind them.

The next moment Eugenia had flown across the hall to Lady Chandross and was dragging her into the opposite saloon.

"Gussie! What *is* it?" she demanded. "Who *are* those men? And what are they saying about Gerry?"

Lady Chandross sank down into an armchair.

"I vow I have no patience with women who have the vapours," she declared, "but if I do not have them now myself it will be nothing short of a miracle! My dear, the most dreadful thing! Here is Cecil taking it into his head to turn up *just* when he is not wanted — something about seeing how things are going on here and escorting us to London: you know how ridiculously punctilious he is! — and arriving *just* as those two creatures had appeared on the doorstep —"

"Yes, but who *are* they? And what have they to do with Gerry?" Eugenia insisted.

Lady Chandross shuddered dramatically. "Well, my dear, if you will credit it, they are Bow Street Runners!" she said. "Yes, truly! They have some ridiculous tale of Lord Barnstaple's travelling coach having been held up by a highwayman on the Bath Road and one of his servants having been killed during the robbery, and obviously they believe that Gerry was the man responsible! It is too absurd! As if Gerry would —"

Eugenia was staring at her, her face suddenly very pale.

"But didn't you tell them that Gerry has been here ever since Saturday?" she asked.

"Of course I did! But it appears the wretched thing took place two days *before* that — Where *are* you going?"

But Eugenia waited for no more; before the astonished question had left Lady Chandross's lips she was out of the room and speeding on her way to the stableyard.

She found Richard and Haggart still standing before the stables in amicable conversation, and to the surprise of both pushed them into the saddle-room, which was fortunately deserted, and closed the door.

"I *don't* wish to upset you, Richard," she said in a slightly quavering voice, "but something dreadful has happened and I think you had best go away at once. You see, there are two Bow Street Runners in the house, looking for my cousin Gerald. They say he held up a coach on the Bath Road last week and someone was killed in the robbery."

Richard's dark brows, which a moment before had been lifted in quizzical surprise at the alarmed haste with which she had hurried him inside, drew together abruptly in a frown.

"The devil you say!" he said. "Are you sure of this?"

"*Quite* sure. I have seen the Runners myself. And Cecil is here — he is talking to them now — and Gussie has told them that you are in the house. They are certain to begin looking for you directly, and one of the servants may have seen you coming out here —"

"Now wait a bit, Miss Eugenia!" urged Haggart, who looked quite staggered by this sudden intrusion of death and danger into his stables, where a moment before only the subdued rattle and jingle of harness, a stable-boy's cheerful whistle, and now and then a companionable whicker had disturbed the cool peace of this late spring morning. "You say they're looking for Mr. *Gerald.* 'Tain't Mr. *Richard* did what they say —"

"Yes," said Richard, "and a nice figure I should cut, trying to convince them I am *not* Gerald Liddiard, when I've been living here under that name for almost a week — and, what is more, have been accepted by his family as such! No, Miss

106

Liddiard is right. Unless I am anxious to see the inside of Newgate Gaol before another four-and-twenty hours have passed, I'm best out of this until the real Gerald Liddiard can be found.'' He turned to Eugenia. ''If I might take one of the horses —''

''Yes — do!'' she said instantly. ''And when you've gone as far as it can carry you, leave it at an inn somewhere under a false name; that way no one will be able to connect it with you.'' Her brow puckered suddenly. ''Oh, Richard, I'm sorry! I'm so sorry!'' she said. ''Truly, I never thought I should land you in this sort of hobble!''

''Of course you didn't,'' said Richard. He took her arm and shook it gently. ''But you needn't worry. I've been in tight spots before this. And if I can lose those Runners now, they're certain to pick up the real Gerald Liddiard's trail sooner or later, and when they do that, there will be nothing to connect me with this business any longer.'' He glanced over at Haggart. ''The sorrel, I think,'' he said. ''And quickly, if you please.''

Haggart disappeared with a celerity remarkable in a man of his age.

"But where will you go?" Eugenia demanded anxiously. "You haven't any money, have you? And it won't be safe for you to turn up at Sir John Alloway's now. Your description — or Gerry's, which comes to the same thing — will be posted in every inn in England."

Richard looked down at her troubled face. "Never mind. I shall do very well," he reassured her. "And I should much rather you had no idea where I am going."

"I shouldn't tell anyone!" Eugenia said, a trifle indignantly.

"I'm quite sure you would not. All the same, it won't do, you know. You have been to far too much trouble over me already."

Haggart appeared in the doorway. He was leading the sorrel.

"Quick work!" said Richard approvingly, and moved forward to swing himself up into the saddle. "To the best of your knowledge," he said to Haggart as the sorrel danced in the stable doorway, impatient to be off, "I took the horse out to exercise him and you expect me back within the hour. Good-bye, Miss Liddiard. And thank you both.''

He was gone before either of them could speak a word, clattering swiftly out of the stable-yard in the direction of the long drive leading to the gatehouse and the road beyond.

"There's a braw lad!" Haggart said, shaking his head with a dismal air. "And worth a dozen of Mr. Gerald. Och, it was an ill turn you did him when you brought him here, Miss Eugenia! He's as like to Mr. Gerald as fourpence to a groat, and it's him they'll hang if they catch him —"

"Then they mustn't catch him!" Eugenia said with determination. "Haggart, will you stand with me now and tell those Runners you knew all along that he wasn't Gerry? Of course Lord Chandross will be furious about it and it may cost you your place here, but I promise you I'll do my very best to find you another, and you may have all my next quarter's allowance —"

Haggart said, looking offended, that it wasn't money he needed to make him speak the truth, and he knew half a dozen places that would be glad of his services any time he chose to leave Lord Chandross's employ.

"But those Runners won't believe me — *or* you, Miss Eugenia," he warned her,"if we tell them 'twasn't Mr. Gerald that was here. They'll only think we're trying to protect him."

Which was precisely, Eugenia was soon to discover, what the Runners did think when, having elicited the information from the servants that Mr. Gerald had last been seen going in the direction of the stables, they appeared there in search of him and heard her story of her meeting with Richard Liddiard at the King's Head at Thatcham. They were accompanied by Lord Chandross, who looked, if possible, even angrier than he had done before, and who obviously shared the Runners' opinion that Eugenia and Haggart had made up the unlikely tale out of the whole cloth in order to shield the offending Gerald.

"I don't know what you can have been thinking of, trying to gull those fellows with a Banbury tale like that!" he said to her furiously when he had seen the two Runners go off in hot pursuit of Richard, having garnered as much information as they could about his departure from a taciturn Haggart and a pair of goggle-eyed stableboys. "It is a reprehensible — a *most* reprehensible — thing to do, to attempt to mislead the Authorities in this way! If Gerald is indeed guilty of the commission of this dreadful crime, he will deserve the retribution that falls upon him! I myself shall do nothing to stand in the way of it! He has brought disgrace upon his family in every possible way, and this final blow does not take me by surprise!"

"Yes, but the man they are looking for now *isn't* Gerry; truly he isn't!" Eugenia said earnestly. "He really *is* Charles Liddiard's son, just as I've told you, even though he looks enough like Gerry to be his twin."

"My dear good child," said Lady Chandross, who was glad enough to see her husband's wrath turn in the direction of someone other than herself, "you forget that I myself saw the man, and spoke with him a dozen times. Of course it was Gerry; I could certainly not be mistaken in such a matter! And there are several of the servants, I am sure, who were acquainted with Gerry in the past; not one of *them* has had the slightest doubt that it was he."

In vain did Eugenia point out that Haggart, the only one of the servants who had known Gerald Liddiard well, was quite willing to confirm her story that the man who had been staying at Mere was not he; neither Lord nor Lady Chandross showed the least inclination to believe her. She left them at last and went upstairs, in disgrace, to her bedchamber, where she dismissed Trimmer, who was waiting to help her out of her riding-dress and incidentally to hear the news that was already spreading like wildfire through the servants' quarters, and sat down to consider the situation.

A worse one she could not imagine. If the Runners should find the real Gerald Liddiard, he would certainly stand in danger of the gallows, whether he had actually committed the crime in question or not (and, knowing Gerry, she could not help believing that sheer recklessness might have led him to play the highwayman and sheer bad luck have led to someone's being killed in the process). And if they found Richard Liddiard instead, and he was unable to prove to the Law's satisfaction that he was himself and not Gerald, an innocent man might be hanged. Worst of all, that would be her doing, because if she had not persuaded him to come to Mere no one would ever have thought of holding him responsible for something that Gerald Liddiard had done.

She stood up and began to unfasten the row of buttons that did up her riding-dress. At least, she thought with determination, they would not find Richard if anything she could do would help to hide him from them. And she believed she knew where he had gone.

"The only friend I have left here," he had told her that evening at the King's Head, "is a Yorkshireman named Ned Trice who became a jockey, went to the bad, and now keeps a very disreputable tavern in Tothill Fields.''

It was the one piece of luck, she thought, in the whole affair — that Richard would almost certainly go to London, to Ned Trice and that disreputable tavern in Tothill Fields, and that she herself would be in London on the morrow.

CHAPTER

6

Unfortunately for Eugenia's resolution to begin to search for a tavern in Tothill Fields kept by a former jockey named Ned Trice the moment she arrived in London, she found herself plunged into such a whirl of activity from the instant she set foot inside Lord Chandross's imposing mansion in Grosvenor Square that she had no opportunity to do anything of the kind, and was obliged to give that important matter over entirely into Haggart's hands.

The most pressing business as far as she was concerned, it seemed, at least in Lady Chandross's mind, was to see her provided with a wardrobe suitable for her introduction into the *ton*, and every waking moment of her first few days in London was spent, under the supervision of either Broaddis or Lady Chandross herself, in the showrooms of fashionable modistes and milliners, where she was fitted out with such a bewildering variety of demi-toilettes, promenade dresses, ball-gowns, and bonnets that she scarcely recognised herself any longer when she looked in her glass.

Never before had it reflected an elegant young lady with her silky dark hair cut and curled in the latest fashionable crop and her slender figure displayed to the greatest advantage in a ravishing succession of high-waisted gowns made of fine French cambrics, Indian mull muslins of diaphanous transparency, sarsnets, and drifts of gauzes, all showing the hallmark of her mentor's unerring taste. Frivolous, expensive, and utterly selfish Lady Chandross might be, but she had an encyclopaedic knowledge of fashion. And as it was her fixed aim to see Eugenia off her hands before the Season was out, she was perfectly willing to put that knowledge to use in her behalf, and to make lavish raids upon her husband's purse in that cause as well.

Eugenia herself, who thought she had become inured, during her three years under Lord Chandross's guardianship, to the prodigal expenditure that went on at Mere, was almost appalled by the number of gowns, costing anywhere from fifty guineas for a simple morning frock to three hundred for the Court dress she was to wear for her presentation at the June Drawing-Room, that now hung in the French *garderobe* in her bedchamber in Grosvenor Square. And when she added to them the price that had been paid for the expensive accessories that were to accompany them — Norwich shawls at twenty guineas, silk stockings, Denmark satin sandals, long French kid gloves in lemon yellow and blossom pink and white — she began to feel that if her relations did not stop spending such vast sums upon her, when what she wanted instead was a modest amount that she might give to Richard as soon as she had found him, she would burst with frustration. It was still several weeks until Quarter Day, when her allowance would be paid her, and of course in the present state of affairs there was no valid reason for her to ask for an advance upon it.

But she consoled herself with the thought that, since Haggart had as yet been unable to discover the tavern in which she was convinced Richard must now be hidden, the need for ready cash had not arisen.

One agreeable event that occurred to leaven her anxiety for Richard during those first days in London was her reunion with Miss Amelia Rowntree. She had, in fact, come upon Muffet within eight-and-forty hours after her arrival there, when she had been taken to the Pantheon Bazaar by Broaddis to purchase a net stocking-purse and a spray of artificial white roses, and had found Muffet and her aunt, Mrs. Lighton, at one of the counters upon a similar errand.

Mrs. Lighton, who was a tall, spare woman dressed in the height of fashion but with very little taste, was the wife of a man whose father had made a large fortune in the City, and as she spent a great deal of time and effort in trying to consolidate her somewhat precarious position in the Polite World, she had been quite willing to undertake Muffet's debut into Society. For one thing, her approving eyes said as they rested upon her niece in eager conversation with Miss Eugenia Liddiard, who was related to the sort of people one most wished to know, one made such very useful acquaintances in chaperoning a girl about to *ton* parties. Mrs. Lighton was sure that this meeting with Miss Liddiard would be responsible for Muffet's being asked to at least a pair of balls to which she could not possibly have hoped otherwise to receive cards; she even toyed for a moment with the dazzling possibility of vouchers for Almack's.

But that, she regretfully conceded, was in the highest degree unlikely. Lady Chandross would certainly request those coveted vouchers for her own protégée from one of the Lady Patronesses of that most exclusive of London clubs, and would as certainly receive them, for she counted Sally Jersey and Dorothea Lieven among her intimate friends; but that Eugenia would be able to persuade her to do the same for Muffet was another matter altogether.

Mrs. Lighton would have been quite willing to suspend her shopping so that Muffet might have an opportunity to talk for as long as she pleased with Miss Liddiard, but Broaddis, with a fitting at a Bruton Street modiste's on her mind, soon swept Eugenia away, and it was not until the following evening at the Dalingridges' ball that the two girls had an opportunity for a more extended conversation.

Even then opportunity had to be seized, for Lady Chandross, who was nothing if not thorough in her efforts to see to it that some eligible young man was enticed, dazzled, or dragooned into offering marriage to her young relation, used all her social arts to make sure that a constant stream of gentlemen of every size and complexion came up to Eugenia, made their bows, and requested her to stand up with them for the next dance. A girl with no fortune, Lady Chandross knew, would be shunned like the Black Death by the sheeplike herd of eligible men, particularly if she was not a beauty in the accepted sense, but an unusual girl, outspoken, quite unflirtatious, and with those alarmingly honest eyes that seemed somehow, even more alarmingly, to demand an equal honesty from one in return; or she would be shunned, that is, unless it could be demonstrated to them from the start that she was to be a belle.

And, thank heavens, Lady Chandross thought, the girl was in looks this evening, with that odd radiant glow in her ordinarily rather cool and matter-of-fact face that made one forget that her features were not in the least classical. And the gown she had chosen for her had certainly been an inspiration — a dress of pale lemon-coloured crape worn over a slip of white sarsnet, which made the pinks and blues of the other young girls appear somehow insipid beside it.

Among the gentlemen so carefully garnered by Lady Chandross for her protégée there was one of whom she had particular hopes. He fulfilled all the necessary criteria — good family, but not so good as to expect to marry a fortune on the strength of his bloodlines; sufficient energy and ambition to do well in the political world with the proper backing; and the kind of agreeable nature that can always be coerced by ruthless people into doing exactly what they wish it to do. The name of this young paragon was Perry Walford, and he was the son, as Lady Chandross had disclosed to Eugenia at Mere, of an old friend of Lord Chandross's who lived in Surrey.

Mr. Walford, presented by her to Eugenia, dutifully asked the latter to stand up with him for the set of country-dances that was forming and, having led her on to the floor, performed with a good deal of concentration his part in the Terpsichorean exercise that followed. Being a rather stocky young man, he began to perspire uncomfortably under the combined influences of an overheated room, very high shirt-points, and his own exertions, and Eugenia, used to handling nervous horses who made a great piece of work over performing some simple action, rather wished she might have him at the end of a lunge-rope, where she felt it would be a good deal easier to show him what he was to do.

Mr. Walford, evidently sensing her slight disapproval of his performance, said to her rather miserably after a while that he dared say she could see he wasn't much of a dab at dancing.

"Oh, I don't know," Eugenia said kindly. "You'd do much better, I expect, if you didn't try quite so hard. Do you hunt?"

Mr. Walford, looking somewhat startled by this change of subject, said that he hunted a little, when he had the chance, but his father didn't keep much of a stable.

"Well, it's like rushing your fences," Eugenia explained. "You're in too much of a hurry to do everything. There's plenty of time. What part of Surrey do you come from?"

Mr. Walford said near Guildford, and, encouraged by Eugenia's friendly manner, told her all about his large family of brothers and sisters, of which he was the youngest, and about his present position as secretary to Lord Dalingridge, which would have been prized by many young men because there was almost nothing to do, but left Mr. Walford, to continue the equine metaphor, champing at the bit.

"If only," he confided to her, "he would speak now and then in the Lords, and ask me to write reports for him beforehand and look up things, it would be a lot jollier. As it is, I'm left kicking my heels most of the day. Your cousin's secretary," he went on enviously, looking at Lord Chandross, who was doing a duty-dance with Lady Dalingridge and looked as if he wished he were somewhere else, "must be awfully busy all day long."

"Yes, I expect he is. Cecil is always making speeches," Eugenia agreed. "Why don't you go and talk to him when the set is over and more or less hint that you'd like a position where there's a lot to do? He knows simply hundreds of people in politics."

But from this proposal Mr. Walford, somewhat to her surprise, shied in evident dismay. The reason for this was simple: he himself had received several hints from his mama, upon the occasion of his last visit to Surrey, to the effect that it would be very nice if he were to see something in London of Lord Chandross's young cousin, Miss Liddiard, who was being brought out that Season — a remark that had been followed by some vaguely pointed reflections upon how rapidly young Bolton, who had married a second cousin once removed of Lord Chandross's upon the maternal side, had risen in the political ranks once he had become a connexion of that eminent peer.

All of this had alarmed Mr. Walford so much that he would probably not have asked Eugenia to stand up with him at all if he had not been outmanoeuvred by Lady Chandross, who had got hold of him and kept him ruthlessly in conversation until the set that had been in progress at the moment had ended and Eugenia had been returned to her by her partner. The next thing he had known, he was walking onto the floor with Eugenia; but he still had no intention of being led sheeplike to the slaughter, despite the fact that he had already revised his original, sight-unseen opinion of Lord Chandross's young cousin and now considered her a capital sort of girl, quite as pretty as any he had ever seen, and he meant to resist strenuously any attempt by her now to lure him into Lord Chandross's clutches.

Eugenia, however, who was much better at dragooning than at luring, made no attempt to use subtlety upon him, but only remarked tolerantly that she didn't much blame him, because Cecil would prose on forever if he once began on politics. She then fell, literally speaking, into Muffet's arms as the set ended, and bore her off into an anteroom on the pretext that she had torn the flounce of her skirt, but really to have an extended talk with her, much to the annoyance of Lady Chandross, who had got hold of a young cornet in the Hussars for her for the next set and didn't know where she had gone.

The anteroom was inhabited, when Eugenia and Muffet entered it, by a Lifeguardsman with very dashing black moustaches and a not so young lady in celestial blue, who had just got themselves nicely settled upon a *tête-à-tête* upholstered in yellow satin; but such was the power of Eugenia's determination not to yield ground, since going outside again would have meant being seized upon by Lady Chandross, that the army realised the futility of resistance almost at once and ignominiously retreated.

"That's better," Eugenia said, as the celestial-blue draperies and the dashing uniform disappeared from view. She pulled Muffet down beside her upon the vacated *tête-à-tête*. "I've a great deal to tell you and there isn't much time. Only first you must promise not to breathe a word of it to anyone else."

Muffet, whose loyalty had been tested over the years at Miss Bascom's to the extent that Eugenia would have been willing to rely upon it even if that mild-mannered preceptress had announced she was about to make use of the rack and thumbscrew to extract information from her, halted the words of admiration she had been uttering for her friend's fashionable appearance and swore secrecy, wide-eyed.

"Well," said Eugenia, "that's all right then. I expect you've heard about my cousin Gerry, haven't you? That he's supposed to have taken to the highroad and killed someone in a robbery?"

Muffet had indeed heard about Gerald Liddiard. Everyone in London, in the *ton* and out of it, had done so by this time — much to the fury of Lord Chandross, who was considering bringing suits for libel against several London journals that had seized upon his relationship to his reckless young kinsman to publish unkind political cartoons about him.

"Yes, of course I've heard about it," Muffet said. "But I expect he is really innocent, isn't he? Gerry wouldn't —"

"Well, I don't know about that," Eugenia said judicially. "I remember his saying that he would like to try everything at least once, so he might have done. Taken to the highroad, that is. Not that he meant to kill anyone, I'm quite sure. But the thing is that, whether he is innocent or not, the Runners are after the

128

wrong man now."

And she proceeded to give Muffet a succinct account of the rather sensational events in which she had had a role since she had parted from her so recently in Bath.

Muffet listened with rapt interest, entirely oblivious by this time to the fact that she was attending her first London ball, that she had not had enough partners to qualify her as even a mild success, and that her aunt was acidly disappointed with her.

"Oh, Eugenia!" she breathed when her friend had concluded. "It's *just* like a book! Are you going to rescue him?"

"Well, I shall certainly try," Eugenia said. "After all, I was the one who got him into this. And I think I know where he is now, only I can't get away from Gussie long enough to go and find out. That," said Eugenia, fixing Muffet with a general's commanding gaze, "is where you come in. You will have to tell Gussie that you have asked me to go for a walk in the park with you tomorrow, and then I can try to find Richard instead."

Muffet, who would as soon have thought of demurring to this somewhat risky project as Flora Macdonald would have considered refusing her aid to Bonnie Prince Charlie, promptly said that she would say anything Eugenia wished her to, only what if Lady Chandross found out it wasn't true?

"Oh — that. If she does, I'll tell her I had an assignation with a man," said Eugenia in a matter-of-fact voice.

Muffet gasped. "But wouldn't she be *furious* —?"

"Oh, yes — but only because I'd be damaged goods if it got about. She's always warning me not to do anything rash until she's succeeded in getting me properly married off. After that, and I've produced an heir, I can do as I like — just as she does. You must say one thing for Gussie; she's *not* a hypocrite."

Muffet was so awed by this speech, foreshadowing as it did a Eugenia whom she might see transformed in the space of a short year from the familiar schoolgirl she had known to a woman of the world carrying on dashing *affaires* with a series of vaguely envisioned gentlemen, all of Brummell-like elegance, with quizzing-glasses at the ready for glimpses of a well-turned ankle, that she almost forgot to ask what hour she was to say.

"Ten, I think," said Eugenia. "Gussie won't be up until noon, and I can be back by then. She'll send me to your aunt's house in Green Street in the carriage, and I can go inside, and then, when we've set off together for our walk, I'll take a hackney cab and go to find Richard. Is your maid trustworthy? I can't possibly take Trimmer."

Muffet said she hadn't got a maid, but her aunt would no doubt send hers to accompany them, and that she — that is, the maid — loathed Mrs. Lighton to the extent that she would be happy to hold her tongue about any odd goings-on, if only to spite her.

"And one thing more," said Eugenia. "Have you any money?"

Muffet, who was of a frugal nature, always had money, and she professed herself quite willing to make a loan of three pounds — which was the extent of her present funds — until Quarter Day.

"It's for Richard," Eugenia explained. "He hasn't any money, you see, or hardly any. Of course he won't like taking it, but he'll have to have something to live on until this affair is cleared up. You can give it to me tomorrow. And now tell me about Tom."

"About Tom?" Muffet, whose mind was on murders and gallows and hairbreadth escapes, blinked at this prosaic intrusion of her brother's name into the conversation.

"Yes," said Eugenia impatiently. "We haven't much time, you know. Gussie or your aunt will be certain to come looking for us before long. Did you talk to him about marrying me?"

Muffet, looking suddenly conscience-stricken, said after a moment that she had tried.

"What do you mean — tried?" Eugenia demanded. "He was there at the Manor, wasn't he?"

Muffet said rather miserably that yes, he had been there all the while. "But I don't think he particularly wants to talk about getting married," she defended herself. "I mean, I couldn't —"

Eugenia looked at her half-tolerantly, half-scornfully. "Oh, very well, I shall talk to him myself," she said, "as soon as I can get down to Kent. But it's rather a nuisance not having it settled now. It's ten to one that Gussie will grow tired of chaperoning me about to parties soon, and then she and Cecil will be dinning it into my ears night and day that I ought to marry one of the young men she has been parading out for me all evening. It would be much more comfortable if I could tell them it was settled between me and Tom."

Muffet said unhappily that she was sorry, which caused Eugenia to tell her not to be a ninnyhammer and to ask her if she was enjoying the ball.

"Oh, excessively!" said Muffet, with a not very convincing show of enthusiasm. "I have never seen so many elegantly dressed people in my life! London is not at all like Kent — is it?"

"I expect," said Eugenia, looking at her percipiently, "you have not had enough partners. Come along; I'll introduce you to some of mine. They're a pretty poor lot, on the whole, but there are one or two who aren't bad.''

And she bore the protesting Muffet off to the ballroom again, where she at once seized upon Mr. Walford — who, had she but known it, was wondering whether he was falling in love with her and considering the daring step of asking her to stand up with him for a second dance — and had the satisfaction of seeing him lead her friend onto the floor before Lady Chandross descended upon her with a captive viscount.

CHAPTER

7

On the following morning, well before ten, Eugenia had had her breakfast and gone out to the mews behind Chandross House to look for Haggart.

"Well, I've found that tavern, Miss Eugenia, but our man's not there," was his greeting to her as she entered the stables, where he was brooding over one of the carriage-horses he suspected of coming down with bog spavin. "And mind your fine clothes now," he added, looking disapprovingly at the fashionable walking-dress of French blue lustring that she had donned for her expedition to Green Street.

Haggart disapproved of finery on principle.

Eugenia, however, paid no heed to the admonition. "How do you know he's not there?" she asked, her heart sinking at this news of failure.

"How do I know? Because I've seen your Ned Trice. He keeps the Fighting Cock in Duck Lane, and nary hide nor hair has he seen of Mr. Richard Liddiard."

"Did he tell you that?"

"He did."

"But, Haggart —!" Inspiration dawned suddenly "Of course he wouldn't! He probably took you for a Runner."

"Me? A Redbreast?" Haggart gave her a disgusted look.

"Well, why not?" argued Eugenia. "You *might* have been. I daresay real Runners don't say who they are when they are trying to track down a criminal."

Haggart grunted, and ran his hand over the big chestnut's hock.

"A shifty little man he is," he said. "A man I'd not trust as far as from here to that door."

"Well, if he *has* got Richard at the Fighting Cock and won't say he is there, I daresay he is trustworthy enough. I think

I had best go to see him and ask. He can't think that *I'm* a Runner.''

Haggart looked horrified. "Mercy-be-here, Miss Eugenia, you'll never!" he said. "Go to a place like that! A young lady like you!" He looked into her determined face and said, with an obvious wrench of principles, for it was quite against his code to have dealings with the enemy, "You tell me this minute you won't do any such thing, or I shall have to go to Lady Chandross!"

"Is it a very bad sort of place?" asked Eugenia, temporising.

"Yes!"

"Oh, very well. I'll think about it then," she remarked noncommittally, and went off before he could press her for further assurances.

But she had not the least intention of giving up her project, and half an hour later, having been conveyed in Lady Chandross's barouche to Mrs. Lighton's house in Green Street, she was telling Muffet all about it while they walked together towards Hyde Park, accompanied at a discreet distance by

Mrs. Lighton's maid.

"I shall be back in Green Street by twelve," she said. "If I'm not, you must just make up some sort of story to fob them off; say I met a girl I knew from Miss Bascom's and went to have an ice with her at Gunther's — oh, you know the sort of thing." At Miss Bascom's it had always been Muffet who had had to provide the explanations for their joint infractions of the rules. "Look — there's a hackney cab!"

And before Muffet could give voice to her misgivings, which were beginning to be quite as lively as Haggart's, Eugenia had signalled the jarvey, had given him, much to his astonishment, instructions to take her to Duck Lane, and was being driven off to that unprepossessing neighbourhood.

Eugenia knew very little about London, and she was perfectly unfamiliar with the sort of squalor she saw about her as the hackney progressed through the noisy, swarming streets that led to her destination. The jarvey, who seemed to be in a very dubious state of mind about her, and was indeed divided between warning her of the hazards of her expedition and telling her flatly that the only place he would take her was back to her home, wherever that might be, decided at last on the former course as he drew up before a low, tumbledown building sporting the sign of a fighting cock painted on a very dirty board over its door.

"Now, missy," he said to her earnestly, "this is the Fighting Cock, but if you was to ask me — which you ain't — I'd say it was no fit place for you. Best let me take you back where you came from."

"Well, you may do that in a very little while," Eugenia said, "but first I must go inside and make some enquiries." She looked about with interest at the grim black houses, nearly all of them with their doors open to reveal their squalid interiors, which appeared to be inhabited chiefly by quarrelling women and screaming babies. A knot of older children, attracted by the unusual sight of a hackney cab with a young lady inside it, had already gathered before the Fighting Cock's door, and a baked potato vendor now left his trade and a cobbler his stall to swell their ranks.

The jarvey, jumping down from his box, gave up his attempts to prevent Eugenia from descending from his vehicle and cleared a way for her to the door, promising meanwhile to await her return. Eugenia thanked him, cast a friendly glance upon her assembled audience, and entered the Fighting Cock's low black door.

She was at once accosted, almost before she had crossed the threshold, by a small, spare man in corduroy breeches and grey stockings, with dirty shirt-sleeves emerging from his unbuttoned waistcoast, who demanded in a very suspicious voice what she wanted.

"Are you Ned Trice?" Eugenia countered.

"Wot if I am?"

"Well, if you are, I should like very much to have a talk with you. In private," she added, looking round at the cobbler, the baked potato vendor, and the ragged children, who were all peering in now at the open doorway.

"Wot about?" Mr. Trice demanded truculently.

Eugenia shook her head. "I said, *in private*," she said firmly. She pointed towards a door that led from the passage in which they stood to the empty taproom. "Can't we go in there?"

Mr. Trice, capitulating, grudgingly led the way inside and closed the door.

"That's better," Eugenia said approvingly. "You see, what I have to say to you is really very confidential." She paused a moment, facing his mistrustful eyes, which were, she saw, almost as yellow as a cat's. "I am Richard Liddiard's cousin," she said then. "Eugenia Liddiard. Is Richard here?"

The yellow eyes narrowed a little — more like a cat's than ever, Eugenia thought.

"Here! Wot are you up to?" the man said roughly. "Yer cousin, is it? Is it likely there's any flash culls in this ken?"

"If you mean any gentlemen, no, it's not very likely," Eugenia admitted, "but it *is* possible. Richard told me you were the only friend he had left in England, and so

141

when he got into trouble I thought of looking for him here. You see, *I* was the one who got him into that trouble, which is the reason why I *must* try to help him now. *Is* he here?"

She looked hopefully at Ned Trice, whose suspicion was evidently giving way now to astonishment.

"Wot kind of help was it you had in mind?" he enquired cautiously, after a moment.

"Money, for one thing," said Eugenia promptly. "I haven't very much now, but I shall have more soon. And if it isn't safe for him to be staying here, I think I know of a better place. My old nurse lives in a cottage on the river near Putney, all alone, and she'd do anything for a Liddiard. No one would think of looking for him there."

She paused, giving Mr. Trice time to digest this information. He considered it for some minutes, during which a slatternly young woman with a baby at her breast opened the door and came in, demanding a penn'orth of gin. Her eyes widened as they fell upon Eugenia; she

142

examined her from her fetching Villager hat to her neat French kid sandals and then, moving forward, held out her hand and in a beggar's whine asked for money.

"I'm sorry, but I haven't any to spare just now," Eugenia said, and added, "I expect it's no good telling you that you oughtn't to be spending the little you have on gin," with a philosophy born of her experience with country shiftlessness, which was not, she considered, so different after all from city shiftlessness.

The woman muttered an ugly epithet, and was at once peremptorily ordered out of the taproom by Ned Trice, who appeared to have made up his mind about Eugenia during this interchange, but not to the extent of accepting her bona fides completely.

"Let's say — jest for the sake of argyment," he remarked, eyeing her cautiously, "that I might be able to find out where this cousin of yours is. Would there be anything you might be wanting me to give him?"

"No. I should like to see him myself, please," Eugenia said definitely. "And it really would be better if you were to take me to him at once, because if I am not back in Green Street by noon it's likely a fuss will be made. Is he here in this house?"

Ned Trice gave up. With a few pithy comments on swell-morts mucking into matters they'd do better to leave in the hands of them as knew what they were doing, he led the way out of the taproom and up a flight of narrow, littered stairs, then up an even darker, narrower flight to an attic under the slates, where he played a complicated tattoo with his knuckles on a battered door.

There was the sound of a bolt being drawn back and the door opened.

"Oh, Richard," said Eugenia to the shirt-sleeved young man who appeared in the doorway, "it's me. May I come in?"

She was, in fact, already being urged inside by Ned Trice, who quickly followed her, closed the door, and shot the bolt to again.

"Keep yer voice down," he growled at her, and looked at Richard Liddiard.

144

"This flash-mort says she's yer cousin," he said.

He had need to go no further; the expression upon Richard's face told him all he wished to know. There was no surprise in it, only a kind of grim and admiring resignation.

"Eugenia," he said. "I might have known. I've cursed myself a thousand times for ever mentioning Ned's name and this place to you."

"Well, it is a very good thing you did, because I never would have been able to find you if you hadn't," Eugenia said practically. Her eyes took in the tiny, low room, with its few sticks of deal furniture and its single small window looking out on the slates, and then went to his face, which seemed almost as pale as it had been when she had first met him at the King's Head in Thatcham. "I shouldn't think you would be very comfortable here," she said.

"Not comfortable," Ned Trice said emphatically, "and not safe, neither. But it's better than Rumbo."

"Rumbo?"

"Newgate," Richard interpreted.

"Ay, and *that's* better than the Nubbing Cheat," said Mr. Trice, by which Eugenia understood him to mean the gallows. He looked at her. "If you've the pitch and pay to get him out of the country, little lady," he said, "give it to him, for the love of God. I'm off downstairs. I mustn't be missed."

And he unbolted the door again and unceremoniously departed.

Eugenia looked at Richard. "I'm afraid I have only three pounds with me today," she said, opening her reticule. "But I shall have more on Quarter Day, if you can wait that long."

She held out Muffet's notes, but Richard made no move to take them.

"Thank you," he said. "But I'm not going anywhere. And I don't need your money. Now you'd best get out of this. How did you come here?"

"I took a hackney cab," said Eugenia. She gazed at him uncertainly, deciding that he could look very intimidating when he chose. "Are you savage with me because I got you into this?"

she ventured.

"Good God, no! It was entirely my own decision to go to Mere. But I *am* angry with you for coming here. You are to have nothing further to do with this business. Is that understood?"

Eugenia's eyes met his equally. "Yes, I understand," she said. "But it's really not fair. Whatever you may say, it *is* my fault that you have got into this hobble, and I'd like to help you out of it. I have been thinking, and it seems to me that if you can get back to Ireland —"

"I have no intention of going back to Ireland."

"Oh?" Eugenia looked at him doubtfully. "Why not? You could be Richard Liddiard quite easily there, couldn't you? Among people who knew you? No one would think you were Gerry there."

"And run the risk for the rest of my life of being taken up for murder if I ever set foot in England again?" Richard said.

He walked over to the window and stood looking out at the forest of grimy chimney pots outside, and, as if she could see inside his head, she suddenly thought, "He is thinking about Coverts. He is thinking that if he can't come back here he can never have Coverts."

"But you — you can't stay here forever," she began rather uncertainly, after a moment.

"No." He had turned back to her again now, a quite unreadable expression upon his face. "That won't be necessary. Not after I've found Gerald Liddiard and seen him turned over to the Authorities." He saw her flinch a little and said roughly, "I'm quite aware you don't like that. But it's the only way I can ever be clear of this business myself."

"But he didn't *mean* to kill anyone. I'm perfectly sure of that," Eugenia said earnestly. "That wouldn't be at all like Gerry."

"I can't help that. It's his neck or mine, and I don't much fancy going to the gallows for a crime I had nothing to do with."

She looked at him, acknowledging with her mind (she was nothing if not logical) that he was right; but something even more powerful (she was also nothing if not loyal) informed her that, no matter how right he was, she could not help him to the extent of aiding him to find Gerald Liddiard. She had not particularly cared for Gerry in the years when she had known him well — he had been charming and selfish and impertinent, always able to put himself in the right even when you helplessly knew him to be quite wrong — but he was a Liddiard and, whatever he had done, she could not be a party to bringing him to the gallows.

She made a small, negative motion of her head, and Richard, who had been watching her intently, said, as if to cap the matter, "He's in London now. I've been able to learn that much. That's why I must stay here. And now," he went to the door and opened it, "you are going. And you won't come back — do you understand?"

"I shall come if you need me," Eugenia said, in the tone in which she might have said, "My name is Eugenia Liddiard," stating the obvious. "But I *can't* help you to find Gerry. Are you sure you won't take the money?"

"Quite sure." His hand rose for a moment and flicked the brim of her fashionable hat. "Don't let them spoil you," he said, smiling at her a little for the first time since she had come into the room.

"Oh, no. It's only the clothes." She looked down disparagingly at the French blue lustring frock. "You wouldn't believe how much they cost."

"Does Tom approve?"

"Tom?"

"Your future husband."

"Oh!" said Eugenia. "I haven't seen him yet. But I expect he wouldn't notice."

The conversation appeared to be over; he was closing the door. She went downstairs and found Ned Trice loitering in the ground-floor passage, obviously on the watch for her.

"Well?" he said.

"He wouldn't take the money," she said, "but perhaps he will from you, if he needs it." She opened her reticule, took out Muffet's three pounds again, and handed the notes to the astonished Ned.

"And if you should ever wish to get in touch with me," she went on, "you might send a message to Haggart, our head groom, at Chandross House. That's in Grosvenor Square. He'll see that I get it."

Ned was looking at the notes, bemused. "Eh," he said, "if that don't beat all hollow! How d'ye know I won't go off and spend every last meg of it on myself?"

"Oh, no," said Eugenia seriously. "I am sure you won't do that. You wouldn't be hiding him here if you didn't care quite as much as I do about getting him out of this trouble."

"Well, it's a rare scuddle he's got himself into," Ned admitted, "and you're right about Ned Trice — he won't buckle. I'd do a deal for Mr. Richard —"

"You've known him for a long time, I expect?" Eugenia asked.

"Since he was no bigger nor a porriwiggle. I was groom to the Reverend Mr. Castle who brought him up, and anything he knows about horses," he said proudly, "he had from me. I've rid at Newmarket and Goodwood in my time, I have."

"Have you? That's very interesting," said Eugenia with sincerity, but added, coming back to the main point at once, "Why isn't it safe for him to stay here?"

Ned's thin shoulders rose expressively. "Eh, missy, you've only to look about you," he said. "Nary a man, woman, or child here in Duck Lane but would whiddle the scrap on him to the Law if they knew there was a ha'porth of gin in it for them. And he *will* go out at night, seeking the man that put him here." London fell from his speech; he said in pure Yorkshire, "I'm that nattered with it all, I'm fretting from morn till night like a fly in a tarbox!"

His harassed yellow eyes met Eugenia's. A very trustworthy cat, she decided, and told him more about her old nurse's cottage on the river.

"I shall go to visit her tomorrow and tell her how matters stand," she said. "Then if things should become really desperate, you can send Richard there. It's a very quiet place; he'd be quite safe, I am sure."

She took her leave of him, passing out

through the Fighting Cock's low black door to where the jarvey stood defending his horse against the attentions of the half dozen urchins who were still waiting outside for her reappearance. Each, she thought, looking with misgiving at the sharp, shrewd little faces, a potential threat to Richard if it became known that he was hidden upstairs in that tiny room under the slates. Meanwhile, she herself had accomplished nothing by her visit to the Fighting Cock except to bring some totally unwanted notoriety upon it.

Eugenia sighed and got into the hackney cab. And what, she asked herself, was she to do next?

CHAPTER

8

As far as Lady Chandross was concerned, what she was to do next was to go to another ball, this one a masquerade, held that evening at a great house in Chiswick. It was, perhaps, not precisely the sort of entertainment to which a young girl just making her come-out would ordinarily be taken by her chaperon, as the host and hostess moved in what proper matrons characterised, with a slight primming of the lips, as the Regent's set, adding that it was unfortunately not to be hoped that quite *all* the gentlemen the Prince distinguished by his notice would keep the line upon such an occasion. There would certainly be a good deal of raking and romping going on under cover of all those masks and dominoes, they informed one another behind their fans at the more innocuous gatherings to which they were happy to escort *their* young charges — but Lady Chandross, who was not a proper matron, had found an excuse for allowing her own charge to attend the masquerade in the fact that, no matter what sort of warm flirtations went on there that evening, one could depend upon it that most of the eligible young men in town would be present.

"Not," she confided dissatisfiedly to her husband as she saw Eugenia, attired in an apple-green domino that wholly concealed her gown of orange-blossom sarsnet, led onto the floor for her first dance by a rather plump young Harlequin, "*not* that she is taking the *least* interest in what she is doing, or in any of these young men. Only fancy — young Beardmore called this afternoon to ask her to drive with him to the Botanical Gardens tomorrow, and she fobbed him off because, she said, she was obliged to visit her old nurse! I daresay she will expect me to let her have the carriage for that little excursion! Well, I shan't."

"May as well," said Lord Chandross, casting a jaundiced eye upon his ward, who was dutifully exchanging chitchat with her partner as they waited to go down the dance together. "She'll only take a hackney cab if you don't. Deuced odd sort of girl — never know what she may take it into her head to do next. Comes of bringing her up without the proper female influence. Always told Walter he ought to marry again."

"Walter Liddiard," said Lady Chandross with asperity, "never cared for anything but Coverts and his horses. *And* Eugenia, of course, whom he brought up to be exactly like himself! Look at her now. Naturally she isn't interested in that pompous young bore she is dancing with, but need she look as if she is on a duty visit to a doddering aunt when she talks to him?"

Lord Chandross shook his head gloomily. "Pity," he said. "Fetching chit, too. But you'll never get her off at this rate."

And he walked off, leaving Lady Chandross to seize upon young Mr. Walford, whose sturdy form she had identified beneath his unimaginative black domino with an experience born of attendance at countless masquerades, and manoeuvre him into a position where he was obliged to ask Eugenia to stand up with him for the quadrille.

This was not difficult to accomplish, as Mr. Walford, who was fast progressing to a state of fervent admiration of Eugenia as a girl with no nonsense about her whom one could really talk to, was all too willing to be led into the trap, and thanked Lady Chandross effusively for giving him a clew as to which of the amazing variety of costumes now thronging the ballroom floor concealed the young lady with whom he wished to dance.

Meanwhile, Eugenia, who under ordinary circumstances would have enjoyed the masquerade in the same way that she had enjoyed dressing up for charades at the Manor with Muffet and Tom, was finding it now merely a sad distraction to her preoccupation with the state of affairs at the Fighting Cock in Duck Lane. It had been obvious to her ever since she had arrived back in Green Street from her visit there that Richard must not remain in such a dangerous situation a moment longer than was necessary, and she had come to the conclusion that, as soon as she could arrange with Old Nan (for so she had always called the diminutive Irishwoman, more properly known as Mrs. Minchinton, who had served both as her father's nurse and her own) to receive him at her cottage on the river, she must despatch Haggart with a message for Ned Trice to send Richard there. She trod through the steps of a country-dance, the quadrille, and the boulanger, but her thoughts were not in the brilliant ballroom in which she stood, but in a low attic room up two pair of stairs in a noisome lane in Tothill Fields.

Her own total disinclination towards anything in the nature of a flirtation, rather than Lady Chandross's care for her — for her chaperon had discovered Lord Rushton and was playing Queen Mab, with a great deal of spirit and no regard for incongruity, to his Louis XIV — had preserved her up to this time from participation in the much-censured "raking and romping" that had been going on. But as the boulanger ended she suddenly found an arm about her waist, and a gentleman in a scarlet domino, whom she remembered to have noticed a short time before standing just inside one the doorways, regarding her fixedly, began to bear her away towards that very doorway.

"Oh! Do give over!" she said indignantly, struggling to free herself.

A low chuckle from behind the mask that hid the scarlet domino's face answered her, and a well-remembered voice said, "Eugenia!" in satisfied tones. "I was sure of it," the voice went on. "You raised your mask for a moment as you joined the set — *quite* improper behaviour at a masquerade, m'dear, but then those things can grow deucedly uncomfortable in a hot room —"

The voice paused as Eugenia, who had ceased to attempt to free herself from the masculine arm still encircling her waist, stiffened in amazement and then, as if in a trance, docilely allowed herself to be led through the doorway into a small anteroom.

When they were inside, she turned to stare disbelievingly at the tall figure in the scarlet domino.

"Gerry!" she said. "It *is* Gerry — isn't it? N-not Richard —?"

"Who is Richard?" enquired the scarlet domino, closing the door behind them. "Don't tell me you've set up a flirt already, my good child. The last time I saw you, you were scarcely out of the cradle!"

"It *is* you!" Eugenia sat down abruptly upon a gilt-and-white Sheraton sofa and pulled off her mask. "It *is*! I can't believe it! Don't you *know* the Runners are after you?"

The well-cut mouth under the black mask curved in a rueful smile.

"Of course I know it! That's why I'm here at this confounded masquerade tonight!" said Gerald Liddiard, seating himself confortably beside her. "Couldn't very well walk bang up to the front door of Chandross House and ask Gleaves if Cecil was at home. Wouldn't do at all. Can't trust servants these days. Might go and lay information. I understand there's a reward."

"Yes, there is, but — oh, Gerry, tell me at once!" Eugenia said anxiously. *"Did you do it?"*

"What — put a bullet through some fat flawn of a coachman because I couldn't manage a horse and a cocked pistol at the same time? What do you take me for?" Gerald said indignantly. "Matter of fact, I wasn't even there. It was that rum-top MacGoff —"

"But, Gerry, everyone is saying it was you!"

"Saying it because they don't know what they're talking about," Gerald said definitely. "Fellow borrowed my mare. Borrowed my coat, too. Don't know that he didn't do it on purpose — though I don't think he's enough brains in his cockloft to think of a thing like that. The point is, Barnstaple — he's the man he held up — recognised the mare. Recognised the coat, too — one of Stulz's make —"

"Do you mean," asked Eugenia, who had been eagerly following this very elliptical explanation, "that it was Captain MacGoff — *our* Captain MacGoff from Kent — who held up the coach and shot the man? And he was wearing *your* coat and riding *your* mare? But why did you allow him to —?"

"Wasn't in any case to stop him," Gerald said, looking rather sheepish for the first time. "Matter of fact, I didn't even know he'd gone. Had had a devilish large evening, you see — a glass or two more of Blue Ruin than was strictly called for —"

"You mean you were foxed," Eugenia said severely. "So foxed that you had no notion what was going on. I daresay if you hadn't been, *you* would have joined forces with that horrid MacGoff in holding up Lord Barnstaple's carriage? Gerry, how *could* you —"

"Well, it was only taking back what belonged to us in the first place," Gerald defended himself. "We were gudgeons enough to sit down to play deep basset with him one night, and the fellow fuzzed the cards. Cut up stiff when we accused him of it, and, dash it all, we couldn't prove it. Took a cool five hundred from us on the head of it. So when we got wind he was going to Bath, we thought we'd just stop his carriage on the road and lift enough off him to cover our losses. Fellow's a curst dandy, you know. There was bound to be enough on him in the way of rings and seals and fobs to make up the amount.''

''Only you drank too much and couldn't go, and Captain MacGoff took *your* horse and coat and shot the coachman by accident, and now everyone thinks it is *you* who did it!'' Eugenia finished the tale for him. ''Oh, Gerry, you *are* a gudgeon! You know what sort of man MacGoff is! Papa was used to say he was so horridly low he would have been more at home in a prize-ring than he ever was in a drawing room, and you know Papa wasn't at all particular!''

Gerald looked a little sulky. Even behind the mask, which he had had prudence enough not to remove, as it was quite possible they might be interrupted at any moment, Eugenia could see how different the face was from Richard Liddiard's, in spite of the amazing similarity in feature and colour. There was a kind of good-natured recklessness in the face she was watching now that she had never seen in Richard's, and none of the latter's cool decision of manner was evident in the volatility that characterised everything the young man now seated beside her said or did.

"Lord, infant," was what he said now, in a tone obviously meant to put her in her place, "one knows all sorts of fellows! And MacGoff is prime company — sings a good song, tells a story well, is ready for every rig and row in town —"

"Yes, that is all very well, but he has landed you in a fine bumblebath now!" Eugenia said. "To say nothing of Richard —"

"Richard again! Who is Richard?" Gerald demanded. "And what has *he* to say to anything?"

Eugenia in a few words sketched for him the story of Richard Liddiard's involvement in his present misfortunes.

"Well, I'm damned!" Gerald said wrathfully, when she had concluded. "I'm sorry, Eugenia, but this is enough to make anyone go off on the ear! And you have the brass to rip up at *me* for getting myself into a bumblebath! Where is this bastard of Cousin Charles's now?"

"Well, I shan't tell you that," Eugenia said, "because if you were to go there he would certainly take you in to Bow Street —"

"I should like to see him do it!"

"But I rather think he could, you know," Eugenia said candidly. "He is very strong, even though he has been ill, and *quite* determined to deliver you up to justice so that he will not be obliged to go on hiding forever merely because he resembles you. It is a horridly awkward situation for him, you see!"

"Well, it is just as awkward for me!" Gerald said, with some asperity. "In fact, this makes it even worse, because if *he* is careless enough to let himself be picked up by the Runners, *I* shall be obliged to turn myself in! Wouldn't do to let an innocent man go to the gallows, even if he is an encroaching upstart who has no more right to call himself a Liddiard than I have to call myself the Prince Regent! Not that I'm not just as innocent as he is, if it comes to that!''

''Yes,'' put in Eugenia, who had been thinking. ''And that is why it appears to me that it would be better if you *did* turn yourself in to the Authorities now and tell them the truth. *I* believed you —''

''Oh yes, you believed me,'' said Gerald, with some bitterness. ''Because you're a female. Females like to think the best of a fellow. But will some beak-nosed, beady-eyed old snudge of a magistrate believe me? *That's* the question. Come to think of it, will Cecil believe me? What do *you* think?''

Eugenia did think, and was obliged to say honestly, ''I really don't know. He is quite furious with you, you see. He says you have disgraced the family name in every possible way and he will do nothing more to help you.''

''You see?'' said Gerald. ''And that's

what I'll hear, and more of the same, from a magistrate if I can't manage to come up with MacGoff and choke the truth out of him somehow. *Or* that man of his — groom, valet, bully, whatever he calls himself. *He* knows the truth, because he was there with MacGoff the night when it all happened —"

"Where is he now? Where are both of them?" Eugenia demanded.

"Loped off to Kent, by all I can learn. Wouldn't surprise me to hear he's intending to leave the country, though of course there's no need for that as long as it's me the Runners are after. I could find out what he's up to soon enough if I could get down there, but it's a dashed risky business for me to show my face out of doors just now. Wouldn't have come here tonight if I hadn't wanted a word with Cecil. You see, Freddy Smythson — fellow who's been putting me up — has got the wind up rather badly and wants me to sherry off. Had a card of invitation for this masquerade tonight, so I told him if he'd give it me and find me a mask and domino I'd relieve him of my company

167

and try what old Cecil would do for me. Paltry sort of fellow, Freddy. When I think of all the scrapes I've pulled *him* out of —"

"Yes, but this is more than a scrape, Gerry," Eugenia said. She was kicking the heel of her satin sandal absently against the gilt leg of the sofa, doing some concencentrated thinking. "Do you mean," she asked after a few moments, "that you can't go back to Mr. Smythson's house at all?"

"Shouldn't like to. He's been like a cat on a hot bakestone all day. So I told him I'd lope off tonight."

"Without knowing where you *would* go? Oh, Gerry!" Eugenia sighed exasperatedly. "If that isn't just like you! Well, I daresay you had best go directly out to Old Nan's cottage when you leave here, then. You will at least be safe there for tonight, until I can talk to Gussie and find out from her if it will do you the least bit of good to ask Cecil for help —"

"Old Nan! Of course! Now why didn't *I* think of that?" Gerald exclaimed. He regarded her with patent admiration. "It's the very place!"

"Yes, but you can't stop there longer than tonight," Eugenia said, "because Richard isn't in a safe place, either, and I have told his friend that he may send *him* to Old Nan's cottage. Only that won't be for a day or two, so meanwhile, until you can make other plans, you had as well stay there yourself. I am going to visit her tomorrow, and so I shall be able to tell you then what the situation is as far as Cecil is concerned."

Gerald assured her that she was a regular right 'un, and, as they were interrupted at this point by a dashing Cavalier and a demure Mary Stuart, who looked disappointed upon seeing the sofa already occupied, Eugenia hastily resumed her mask and proceeded to speed Gerald on his way.

"I hope you may arrive there safely," she said anxiously; but Gerald said confidently that there was no doubt of that. It was a dark, moonless night and he would go by the river; with his hat pulled well over his eyes, it was hardly likely

that any sleepy waterman would so much
as see what he looked like, far less
recognise him as a wanted man.

CHAPTER
9

Approximately an hour before this conversation took place a tall young man in an olive-green coat, with his hat pulled well over his eyes, walked down from the embankment to Westminster Steps, where he engaged a waterman to row him up the river to Putney. A light fog was already rising from the dark water, half-obscuring the flickering light of the flares at the foot of the steps; there were only a few people about, as the hour was past eleven, and neither they nor the yawning waterman paid any particular heed to the tall young man as he settled himself in the slender craft.

The waterman dutifully rowed him past

the lights of the city, past Vauxhall and Chelsea, until grassy banks shadowed by dark-looming shapes of beech and oak, small farmhouses, each with its path leading down to the river, and a tangle of overgrown vineyards took their places. The young man was taciturn; the waterman continued to intersperse his labours with yawns. The creak and rattle of the oars in the oarlocks sounded very clear in the still foggy air.

At length, just before the wooden bridge at Putney was reached, the young man indicated one of the rickety jetties, with a single small boat riding beside it, that ran down to the river's edge. The waterman pulled in to it; the young man paid his fare and, as the waterman rowed himself off again into the damp mist, disappeared up the fog-shrouded path.

The path led to a stile in a hawthorne hedge, and thence by a flagged walk to a small, neat cottage with a thatched roof and mullioned windows, the darkness surrounding it fragrant with the scent of the white ramblers growing thickly about its porch. The young man knocked upon the weathered oak door. There was no response from within, but as he knocked again a large white cat materialised silently in the foggy darkness from around the corner of the house and sat down a few feet away from him on the path, aloof but companionable.

The young man swore softly. He was about to attack the door for the third time when there was a rattle of bolts from inside and it opened abruptly to reveal a very diminutive elderly female, whose nightcapped head scarcely topped his elbow. She was carrying a candle, and held it up at once to examine his face.

"Waking a body up in the middle of the night!" she said severely, evidently continuing a monologue that had begun long before she had unbarred the door to him. "I never heard of such a thing in all my days! What do you want? Speak up now, young man, and don't stand there gawking like a looby! Who are you and what do you —?" Her voice died away suddenly; her sharp black eyes opened wide. "Master Gerald!" she said, in the voice that had sounded doom to

173

generations of Liddiard nurselings. *"Master Gerald!* You come inside this very minute! And *don't* forget to wipe your feet!"

The tall young man, however, did not step across the threshold.

"It's not Gerald; it's Richard," he said. "Didn't Miss Liddiard — Eugenia — tell you —?"

"I haven't set eyes on Miss Eugenia these nine months and more," Old Nan snapped. "And I'll thank you to do as you're told, Master Gerald, and not try any of your May-games on *me. I* know your tricks. You needn't think I don't!"

Thus adjured, Richard Liddiard obediently wiped his feet upon the mat and stepped inside. He found himself in a small, low-beamed parlour, which showed, even in the light of the single candle Old Nan held, a gleam of lovingly polished wood and shining brasses, and an immaculately scoured brick floor. The white cat, stalking in beside him, sprang up upon the settle in the inglenook, lay down comfortably, and awaited events.

"Having those Bow Street Runners

after you — a fine thing for a gentleman!" Old Nan scolded meanwhile, as she set the candle down upon a table and struggled to rebar the door. Richard came to her aid, and as he completed the task and turned about found her standing staring up at him with her mouth open in comical dismay. "Oh!" she said in a shaken voice. *"Oh!* You're *not* Master Gerald! You can't be!"

"No, I'm not. I've been trying to tell you so," Richard said mildly. "But why are you so sure? Eugenia didn't believe me when I told her I wasn't Gerald, and Lady Chandross never suspected."

"Miss Eugenia!" Old Nan sniffed, recovering herself quickly. *"She* didn't know him when he was in short coats. *I* did. Master Gerald 'ud never think of helping me with that door like that." She looked at him suspiciously. "And who *are* you, then?" she demanded.

"I've already told you, I'm Richard Liddiard," Richard said. "Charles Liddiard's son."

"Mr. Charles's son! But —"

"I know, I know. Charles Liddiard

175

never married, so he couldn't have had a son —"

Old Nan bridled. "None of your sauce, young man!" she said tartly. "I dessay I know a Liddiard when I see one! You're as like to Master Gerald as two peas in a pod, with that wicked-looking face on you —"

"Well, I can't help my face, can I?" Richard asked reasonably. "And I'll tell you this, Nannie — right now I'd change it if I could. If I didn't look like Gerald Liddiard I wouldn't have the Runners after me and have to come to you to help me."

"Sauce!" said Old Nan again, picking the white cat up from the settle and dumping it upon the hearthrug as if to relieve her feelings. "You're all alike!" She stood before him, staring up pertinaciously into his face. "Downpin, ain't you?" she demanded. "Fever?"

"I'm all over that now."

"Yes, I can see you are. But gaunt as a churchmouse. Haven't had a good meal in a week, I'll be bound. You wait here."

She stumped off, carrying the candle, and leaving him in the darkness with the white cat, who had decided to be friendly and was rubbing coquettishly against his legs. In a few moments Old Nan returned, carrying a plate with a large portion of raised pigeon pie upon it, which she set down with a thump upon a small table. Richard, who had found the fare at the Fighting Cock decidedly unappealing, was perfectly willing to do justice to it, particularly as he had been obliged, by the news that a pair of Runners had appeared at the front door, to take a hasty departure from one of the tavern windows just as he had been about to partake of the unappetising stew that had been brought for his supper.

Over the meal he told Old Nan something of his history, and was relieved to find that her loyalty to the Liddiard family was not limited by nice considerations of legitimacy. She told him that he was welcome to stay at her cottage as long as he liked, that he would be quite safe there if he could be sure he had not been followed from the town by the Runners, and that she personally would take care of anyone who came nosing round — which latter fact he did not doubt in the least. She then said severely that he would be obliged to sleep on the settle, lugged in a blanket and a pillow for him, and mounted the stairs (she was so small that she took them like a child, planting one foot and then bringing up the other) to her own bedchamber above.

Richard, left alone in the parlour — the white cat having been put out again — arranged his tall frame as comfortably as he could upon the settle and, resolutely putting out of his mind the problem of what he was to do on the morrow, soon fell asleep.

He was awakened from his first slumber a short time later by the sound of a cautious rapping upon the front door. He sat up, threw the blanket aside, and quickly drew on his boots. The rapping continued with increasing vigour, to the accompaniment presently of a low, urgent masculine call of, "Nan! Nan! Wake up! It's Gerry!"

"Of all the impossible luck!" thought Richard.

And he was at the door in a moment, unbolting and unbarring it swiftly; the next instant he had it open and, springing upon the dark figure that stood outside, had dragged it into the parlour.

Gerald, too staggered by this sudden and perfectly unexpected attack to resist for the first moment or two, suddenly came to himself as he found himself being haled into the pitch-darkness of the little parlour, and began struggling furiously to free himself from his unknown assailant. The two men were of equal height and weight, and though Richard, owing to the outdoor life he had led, was, as Eugenia had candidly observed, the stronger, it was not for nothing that Gerald had sparred with Gentleman Jackson himself in the former champion's famous Boxing Saloon in Bond Street. A titanic struggle ensued: chairs went crashing into walls; the settle was overturned with a thump that shook the little cottage to its foundations; there was the ominous tinkle of breaking glass. The combatants were

179

so engrossed in their battle that neither of them noticed flickering candlelight progressing steadily down the stairs, or heard anything but their own fierce, panting breathing until Gerald, neatly thrown on Richard's hip, went sprawling into the fireplace and lay there, stunned.

It was at that moment that Richard became aware of a broom beating erratically upon his legs and of a shrill voice coming from somewhere in the vicinity of his elbow.

"Turning — my — parlour — upside down!" said the shrill voice furiously, punctuating each word with a fresh attack of the broom upon the calves of Richard's legs. "A pair of plaguey — addle-pated — rascals —"

Richard looked down at her. "I'll put it to rights again, Nannie," he said mildly. "Look here, stop that now!" He took the broom from her and leaned it against the wall. "Would you happen to have a piece of rope I could tie this fellow up with?" he asked.

Old Nan stood looking up at him, the very strings of her nightcap trembling with her indignation.

"Tie up Master Gerald!" she said. "The idea! I dessay you've killed him, you great brute! And serve him right! Fighting and rioting in my parlour at this time of night!"

She trod over to the recumbent Gerald, who was already stirring, however, and rubbing what was obviously going to be a large lump on his head. Seeing that he was not seriously injured, she dismissed him contemptuously and began trotting about the room, busily righting fallen chairs, replacing cushions, and clicking her tongue over the remains of a hideous green-and-yellow vase that had been broken in the conflict.

When she attacked the settle, pitting her tiny strength against its immovable bulk as she attempted to right it, Richard perforce came to her aid. Gerald sat up.

"I — say!" he remarked rather thickly, staring up at Richard's face, illumined now by the candle's glow. *"You're Eugenia's Richard."*

"I'm Richard Liddiard — yes," Richard said grimly, looking down at him. "And you and I, Mr. Gerald Liddiard, are now going to make a trip to Bow Street —"

"Don't be a sapskull, man!" Gerald said, holding his head and looking irritable. "*I* didn't put a bullet through that blasted coachman — it was Will MacGoff, just as I was telling Eugenia this evening." He staggered to his feet. "Nan, haven't you a drop of brandy somewhere about? My head's splitting," he complained.

"Serves you right," said Old Nan vengefully. "And I wish his was, too! The very idea! Fighting in *my* parlour!"

She trotted off to the kitchen, and Gerald, collapsing upon the settle, said to Richard in grudging admiration, "Threw me a cross-buttock, didn't you? I'm out of condition or I'd have given you a better run for your money. Too much Blue Ruin, I expect. I say, though," he added, "you're after the wrong man, you know, if you think I was the one who put a hole through Barnstaple's coachman. Fellow named MacGoff borrowed my mare and coat and held up the coach; he was masked, of course, and that's how

Barnstaple came to identify me as the man. Nasty mistake, but there you are."

Richard was looking at him skeptically. "Who is this MacGoff?" he asked.

"Will MacGoff!" Old Nan, coming back into the room with a tumbler in her hand, spoke before Gerald could reply. "*Captain* Will MacGoff!" she repeated scornfully. "A Captain Hackum is more like it! *He's* a nasty piece of work, he is! A great, braggartly make-bait. Mr. Walter never could abide him! If *that's* the sort of company you've been keeping, Master Gerald, it's no wonder to me that you've got yourself into the briars!"

Gerald accepted the brandy with thanks and drank it down.

"Well, it's no good thinking about that now," he said. "The thing is, we shall have to contrive to come up with that fellow by hedge or by stile and get the truth out of him." He looked up accusingly at Richard, who was still standing over him rather menacingly. "By the bye, I dropped in at the Lassiters' masquerade tonight and managed to have a few words with Eugenia. She told me all about *your* little game," he said. "I must say you had an infernal amount of brass, going to Mere and giving out that you were me! You can't blame *me* that you're in this now, too."

"No, I daresay I can't," admitted Richard. "But if you shot that coachman —"

"I keep telling you, I didn't shoot him," Gerald said impatiently. "If you want to know where I was that night, I was asleep in a room in a hedge-tavern near Hounslow. I was a little above par, you see, so MacGoff took my mare and coat and went off after Barnstaple alone, except for that man of his. A little matter of fuzzed cards, it was — that money was due us. And the first I knew of what a dashed mull they'd made of the business was when I came down to the coffeeroom in the morning and found everyone's tongue on the tattle about the holdup, and how Barnstaple had identified the man who'd shot his blasted coachman as Gerald Liddiard. Luckily it wasn't the sort of inn where names are given, so none of them knew *I* was the fellow they were talking about. I hedged off out of there in a flea's leap, I can tell you! Well, it stood to reason I couldn't prove I hadn't been out of that room all night —''

''Shatterbrained — that's what you are, Master Gerald, and always were!'' Old Nan said reprovingly. ''You'd best come in the kitchen with me and let me tend to that head. He's bloodied you. You'll need a bit of court-plaster.''

She tugged him out into the kitchen with her, while Richard, left alone, sat down to think what he was to do now. The goal he had had ever since he had left Mere Court with the Bow Street Runners hot on his heels — to find Gerald Liddiard — had been accomplished; but if Gerald was speaking the truth when he claimed that he had not been present at the holdup, he, Richard, could buy his own safety only at the price of turning an innocent man over to the Authorities.

It was a frustrating situation, especially since on the whole he was inclined to believe Gerald's story. Bow Street, with their man unimpeachably identified by a reliable eyewitness to the crime, might not believe it; but then Bow Street had not had the advantage of seeing Old Nan's reception of her former nurseling's tale. If Gerald had been lying, Old Nan would have been the first to come down on him; but Old Nan had accepted his story without an instant's hesitation or suspicion.

Richard sighed exasperatedly. So it was to be dodging the Runners for him again, he supposed, this time looking for a man of whose very existence he had been happily unaware half an hour before. He wondered what Bow Street would do if he and Gerald both simply gave up the game and surrendered themselves jointly, each claiming to be Richard Liddiard and inviting the Authorities to decide among themselves which of the two was really Gerald. Bow Street could not very well hold two men for a crime that only one of them could have committed, and, barring Old Nan's special powers of perception, it could not possibly know which was the man it wanted.

A tempting solution, he thought, but not one that really offered a permanent answer to the problem. No, he would have to contrive somehow, it seemed, to find Captain Will MacGoff, of whose whereabouts he could only hope that Gerald Liddiard now had some firm idea.

CHAPTER

10

The problem of finding Captain MacGoff was being discussed by Gerald and Richard over ham and toast and buttered eggs in the kitchen of Old Nan's cottage on the following morning when Eugenia arrived, having herself had an unfashionably early breakfast in Grosvenor Square. They were expecting her, as Gerald had informed the others of her intention of paying a visit to her old nurse that morning, so that her appearance occasioned no surprise; but her own astonishment at finding Richard there, apparently sharing an amicable breakfast with the man he had been seeking with the grim intention of turning him over to Bow Street, was obvious.

"Richard! What *are* you doing here?" she exclaimed, and, without waiting for a reply, turned anxiously to Gerald. "Is he going to turn you over to the Runners?" she demanded. "And what has happened to your head?"

"One question at a time," Richard said calmly. "First, I am here because the Runners made a visit last night to the Fighting Cock. Second, I have no present intention of turning your cousin —"

"*And* yours!" Gerald interpolated, grinning.

"— over to the Runners. And third, the court-plaster is decorating his head because we had a slight disagreement upon his arrival."

"A slight disagreement!" Old Nan put in, sniffing. "*I'd* have another word for it, Miss Eugenia! Turned my parlour upside down, they did, and broke that green-and-yellow vase Minchinton brought me back from Yarmouth, to say nothing of putting a great nasty gash in Master Gerald's forehead." She surveyed with an appearance of grudging admiration

189

Eugenia's elegant frock of almond-green cambric muslin and her flat-crowned Villager hat. "I dessay you'll be too fine a lady now to sit down in my kitchen," she said. "There's ham left, and plenty of hot buttered toast."

"Oh yes, *please,* Nan!" Eugenia said happily. "I've already had breakfast in Grosvenor Square, but it is the fashion to be thin, you know, and people *do* look at you so if you do more than nibble at things in a ladylike way!"

"If you was to get any thinner, you'd blow away altogether," Old Nan said scornfully. "I've no patience with people who grudge a growing girl a decent meal."

"Well, I expect I won't grow any more now, but I *would* like some of that ham," Eugenia said, sitting down between Gerald and Richard as Old Nan piled a plate lavishly high. She turned to Gerald. "I'm sorry about your head, but I *did* tell you that Richard was very strong," she said to him seriously. "And I'm sorry, too, that I haven't good news for you about Cecil. I tried mentioning your name to him very cautiously last night as we were driving back to Grosvenor Square from the masquerade. I only said I'd been talking to someone who thought you might have been seen in London. And Cecil said that the sooner Bow Street caught up with you the better, because then people might stop bibble-babbling about you and forget the whole disgraceful business. And when I said if we could find you he might be able to help you to leave the country, he said he would do nothing of the sort, because if he did you would only come back and do something worse — though what could be worse than murder I really can't think. But he was in a very twitty temper, so I thought I had best drop the subject, at least for the time.

"Good God, yes!" Gerald said feelingly. "If he's in one of those moods, he's as like as not to come the ugly and turn me over to Bow Street himself. We shall have to contrive without him — that's plain. You don't by any chance know of a way of getting Richard and me down to Kent without anyone's catching sight of us on the way, do you?"

"No," said Eugenia, helping herself to buttered toast. "You're both too large to put into a bandbox, or even a trunk. But if you do think of a way, I'd like very much to go down to Kent and help you to look for Captain MacGoff myself, because Gussie is beginning to be very wearing about my encouraging Perry Walford to marry me — *Oh*!" She broke off, her eyes suddenly lighting up. "There *is* — that is, there may be — a way, after all! I mean, a way we could all three go. Of course, I should have to have Muffet's help. But no one ever looks at footmen — do they? I mean, all anyone would think was that you both looked alike, and if you are hunting for one criminal, you would never expect to find *two*."

Richard and Gerald exchanged glances.

"Do you," enquired Richard, "have the least idea what she is talking about?"

"Not the faintest," said Gerald cheerfully. "It sounds to me as if she were planning another masquerade, with the two of us cast to go as footmen. And why Muffet?" He turned to Eugenia. "I gather you are alluding to young

Miss Rowntree?''

"Yes. I am going to marry Tom Rowntree, you see," said Eugenia. "That is, I am going to if I can ever manage to get down to Kent to tell him about it."

"*Tell* him about it?" Gerald repeated incredulously.

"Yes," said Richard gravely. "You see, Miss Liddiard considers it unfair that *we* should always be required to do the asking."

"Don't be superior," Eugenia said equably. "And please call me Eugenia." She looked from one to the other of the two handsome, dark-browed faces, so remarkably alike in feature, so remarkably dissimilar in expression. "It is a splendid idea," she said. "Or at least it will be when I have worked it all out. You see, if I tell Gussie and Cecil that Tom wishes to make me an offer, only he can't leave Kent, I think it is quite likely that they will be happy enough to have me off their hands to send me down to Kent for a visit. Then Haggart can borrow the proper livery for you, and you can both come along as footmen."

Richard and Gerald again exchanged glances.

"I can think," Richard said judicially after a moment, "of at least six serious flaws in that plan. Would you like me to name them? In the first place, you have not been invited to visit the Rowntrees —"

"Oh, that doesn't matter. I can always say Mrs. Rowntree wrote, only I have mislaid the letter. And Mrs. Rowntree won't at all mind having me. She is really very fond of me."

"You don't think," Richard enquired, "that it may be a bit awkward trying to explain to her why you are suddenly turning up on her doorstep in the middle of the Season you are presumably enjoying in London?"

"Well, I hadn't thought of that," Eugenia admitted. "But I expect something will occur to me — or to Muffet — before we arrive. She is very good at making up excuses, though you wouldn't think it to look at her."

"Oh," said Richard politely. "Miss Rowntree is to accompany you, then?"

"Well, of course! I couldn't manage it without Muffet. You see," said Eugenia, improvising rapidly between bites of buttered toast, "if I were to try to go alone, I should be sure to have Trimmer foisted upon me, and that wouldn't do at all. But if Muffet comes too, *she* can tell her aunt that Gussie is sending Trimmer with me, and *I* can tell Gussie that Mrs. Lighton is sending *her* maid with Muffet. And then, you see, we shall be able to go without either of them."

She gazed triumphantly at Richard and Gerald, who, in the manner of men, were both looking extremely skeptical about a plan they had not thought of themselves.

"The last time I participated in one of your well-meant schemes, Miss Liddiard — I beg your pardon, Eugenia," Richard said, "it ended with my being pursued by the Bow Street Runners on a charge of murder. That may explain my lack of enthusiasm about this one. If I might point out to you some of the other flaws I see in it — what, for example, will Lady Chandross's coachman think when he is joined by two footmen he has never clapped eyes on before?"

"But he won't be the coachman. He will be Haggart," Eugenia said, ingeniously overcoming this objection as she had the others. "I shall ask Gussie particularly if he may not drive the carriage instead of Suggs, or instead of sending us in the chaise with postillions, because he is anxious to see his sister, who is very ill in Kent —"

"*Has* Haggart a sister, ill or not ill?" Richard asked inexorably.

"No," said Eugenia. "But Gussie doesn't know that."

She looked at him rather guiltily. Gerald broke into a shout of laughter.

"The things Gussie doesn't know, and isn't to know!" he said. "You have certainly come on since I last saw you, infant! How many flirtations are you carrying on now that Gussie doesn't know about, either?"

"None at all," Eugenia said indignantly. "This isn't anything in the least like that. It is a matter of life and death." She looked at him doubtfully. "Do you mean you really don't want to do it?" she asked.

"My dear coz," said Gerald, "I'd do it like a shot if I thought we could carry it off. But —"

"You would both make very good footmen," Eugenia encouraged him. "You are quite of the proper height. Gussie, of course, is so fashionable that she insists upon having footmen who are at least six feet tall, so I am sure their livery would fit you. James, I believe, is obliged to pad his calves, but perhaps you —"

She looked speculatively at the two young men.

"What do you take us for?" Gerald said with some hauteur. "A pair of spindle-shanks? I am sure I can fill out a pair of white silk stockings as well as the next fellow, while as for Richard, no man who is as good in a mill as he is can lack for muscle in his calves or anywhere else."

"Thank you!" said Richard, a trifle sardonically. "And perhaps you, or Eugenia, can tell me what is to be done with this remarkable pair of twin footmen when we reach Kent, where I have no doubt that their features are very well-known —"

"Well, I haven't got round to that yet," Gerald confessed. "Couldn't pass ourselves off as footmen there — that's a fact."

He looked at Eugenia, who had finished her toast and ham and sat regarding him in frowning thought, her chin dropped into her cupped hands. The white cat appeared suddenly in the open casement window, bounded to the floor in a graceful leap, and sat down beside her, looking up hopefully at the scraps upon her plate. Eugenia absently began to feed him. All at once she stopped, her eyes widening triumphantly.

"Lady B.!" she proclaimed.

"What?" said Gerald and Richard simultaneously.

"Lady Brassborough!" Eugenia explained impatiently. "Gerry, you *must* see that she would be the very one! No one ever visits the Dower House — no one who is in the least respectable, at any rate — and her servants don't speak English, you know, besides being as old as

Methuselah and never venturing into the village —"

She looked hopefully at Gerald, who appeared to be considering her words.

"Think she'd have us — eh?" he asked after a moment.

"I'm quite sure she would. She would adore it! You know she has always been fond of you — and of me." She looked at Old Nan, an expression of sudden mischief on her face. "I don't know how many scolds poor Papa had to undergo from Nan because he *would* allow me to visit the Dower House."

Old Nan's nose went into the air. "It wasn't for *me* to tell Mr. Walter how to raise you," she said primly, but with awful emphasis. "But to *my* way of thinking it's the outside of enough to let a Pure Young Girl be taken in the clutches of a Scarlet Woman —"

"Oh, Nan! Lady B. isn't a Scarlet Woman! Or at least she hasn't been for ages — not since she married Lord Brassborough, and he's been dead for a dozen years."

"She was In the Theatre before she

married him," Old Nan said darkly. "Cavorting about showing her legs there, if what's said is to be believed."

Gerald said, grinning, "and a dashed fine pair they were, I'll wager, though she's taken on considerable tonnage since then." He looked at Eugenia. "She might do it, I daresay," he admitted. "Sort of thing she'd enjoy. And you're quite right about our being safe there. None of the servants likely to go tattling in the village."

Eugenia turned to Richard. "I expect I ought to explain to you," she said scrupulously, "that we are talking about the Dowager Lady Brassborough, who was on the stage when she was younger — perhaps you may have heard of her — Meg Morvin? — and lives alone now quite near the Manor with only French servants because she and Lord Brassborough always lived abroad while they were married, and then he died and she came back to live at the Dower House, only to spite the present Lady Brassborough, she says, who is a dreadful prig —"

She paused, rather out of breath from

the long sentence, and looked at him hopefully.

"I think," he remarked conversationally, "you have both run quite mad. When I consider I was always used to wish to make the acquaintance of my noble relations —!"

"Oh, Eugenia and I ain't noble," Gerald said comfortably. "That's only Cecil, and you want to make dashed sure you don't make *his* acquaintance, for you wouldn't care for him above half. And I don't see what call you have to say Eugenia and I have rats in our garrets, for a more caper-witted rig than the one *you* ran at Mere I never heard of. This one ain't half so bad. We'll be as safe as a church at the Dower House once we get down there, and then you and I can nose out that scoundrel MacGoff and see that he comes by his deserts."

He and Eugenia thereupon proceeded to lay their plans for putting her scheme into practice at the earliest possible moment, while Richard, seated in the homely little kitchen with its lattice-window open on a fragrant hedge of briar and honeysuckle, drowsy with bee-hum, began to succumb to a sense of living in a child's safe world of sunlight and adventure instead of within the nightmarish circle of danger that had surrounded him since he had left Mere. They were both children still, he thought, watching them, though Gerald was probably quite as old as he was himself and Eugenia had her own direct and practical wisdom, much beyond her years.

But he himself had once seen a man die upon the gallows, a man he had known and worked with in Ireland; what might be at the end of this business for him or for Gerald Liddiard was no mere child's bogey to him, which would dissolve into safety and laughter once the fright was past.

He saw Eugenia look up at him suddenly, drawn out of the absorption of their planning, it seemed, by his very silence.

"Richard," she said to him earnestly, "you *will* do it — won't you? Really, it will be *quite* safe. You *can't* think I'd ask you to do it if it weren't."

Quite safe, he thought. An outrageous masquerade, depending for its success upon its very brazen audacity, and carried out in complicity with a pair of schoolgirls and a reckless young wastrel.

But it was the only path that offered. He could not remain in hiding indefinitely in Old Nan's cottage, nor, if it came to that, did he wish to leave in Gerald Liddiard's hands the task of bringing into the open the truth of what had happened that night on the Bath Road. It was, by the very fact of his resemblance to Gerald and of his having walked in Gerald's shoes for a week at Mere, certainly his own task as well.

"Very well," he said calmly, as he had said the words once before in a private parlour in the King's Head at Thatcham over a proposal almost as risky as this. "I'm on" — and saw her eyes light up with relief and pleasure.

"Oh, Richard, I am so glad!" she said. "And I'm *quite* sure it will all work out perfectly splendidly."

Gerald said, "Famous!" and Old Nan, disapproving and practical as ever, asked if anyone wanted more ham or toast.

CHAPTER

11

As it developed, Eugenia had been somewhat overly optimistic about the ease with which her plan could be carried into action. Directing the coachman, when she left Old Nan's cottage, to drive her to Green Street instead of back to Grosvenor Square, she had a brief colloquy there with Muffet that had the unexpected result of causing even that heroine-worshipping young lady to fall into a quake, and to declare with fervour that she couldn't, she wouldn't, she was quite sure she could never bring it off, and what in the world could she say to her mama when the two of them turned up so unexpectedly in Kent?

"I *can't* tell her you've come because Tom wants to marry you," she said agitatedly, "because perhaps he doesn't, and he would be so very angry with me if I said he did! Only think what a position it would put him in! He would be obliged to offer for you then, you know!"

"Nonsense!" said Eugenia impatiently. "Of course you needn't say anything at all to your mama about Tom's wishing to marry me. *That* is only what I shall have to tell Gussie so that she will allow me to go into Kent. You must merely write to her that we are both quite fagged to death by all our engagements here in London, and that Gussie and your aunt think it would do us a great deal of good to spend a week or two quietly in the country."

"But Aunt Lizzie doesn't — ! What am I to tell *her?*"

"Tell her Gussie thinks *I* am worn down and you have invited me to visit you at the Manor. And be sure to tell her as well," Eugenia added with worldly-wise knowledge, "that Lord Chandross will be sending us in his carriage. She is awfully fond of a crest, isn't she?"

Muffet admitted unhappily that Mrs. Lighton was indeed very apt to agree to any scheme that brought her or her niece into intimacy with the higher nobility, but she was still so doubtful of being able to carry off the monstrous amount of deception involved in the plan that Eugenia was obliged to promise that she herself would break the news both to Mrs. Lighton and to Gussie about the invitation to the Manor and the mislaid letter.

For a young lady who had professed herself a poor liar, Eugenia reflected, she was getting into some very deep waters indeed, but, consoling herself with the thought that it was all in a good cause and that she must simply consider it as acting, as she had when she had brought Richard to Mere, she went back to Grosvenor Square to beard Gussie in her den.

The den turned out to be her bedchamber, for Lady Chandross was a notoriously late riser and was just finishing her breakfast chocolate amidst the lace-edged pillows and pink silk draperies of that elegant apartment when Eugenia arrived in Grosvenor Square.

Lady Chandross was not in the sunniest of moods, having just received a card of invitation to a particularly intriguing party to be given by a particularly indiscreet peeress, which she wished very much to attend but to which she could not possibly bring Eugenia. Visions of being burdened not only during this Season, but also the next, with a marriageable young relation who refused, against all reason, to allow herself to be married off, were tracing a sulky line between Gussie's brows when Eugenia entered the room. The latter could not, in fact, have chosen a better moment in which to bring forward Tom's as yet fictitious pretensions to her hand.

"Young Rowntree!" she could almost see the thoughts chasing one another through Gussie's head when she had concluded her speech. "*Not* a brilliant match, but certainly an eligible one. A very respectable property, I have heard it said, and he is the only son. Of course he is probably a horrid bumpkin, but one wouldn't be obliged to have them often at Mere. I *don't* think Cecil can object — not

when he has seen how the girl has made
mice feet of every opportunity we have
thrown in her way.''

Aloud she merely said, ''Well, my love,
what a sly thing you are, to be sure! So
this is why you have turned a cold
shoulder to every other eligible *parti* I
have presented to you! Is he very
handsome, your Tom?''

Eugenia, who had never considered the
matter, Tom merely being Tom, whom
one had known since one had been
staggering about in leading-strings, said
after a moment's reflection that she
dared say he was.

Gussie laughed. ''Well, I must say, you
don't sound frightfully ardent,'' she said.
''Not in the least like a girl who is top-
over-tail in love!''

Eugenia hastened to assure her that she
was very fond of Tom, but at the same
moment she was conscious of a peculiar
feeling of uncertainty somewhere inside
her — an extraordinarily disagreeable
feeling, for she was not used to doubting
her own decisions. In a few days, if all
went according to plan, she would be in

Kent and could tell Tom, as she had long been wishing to, all about the advantages of their being married. He would no doubt agree, and a notice would then be sent to the *Morning Post,* setting in motion an inexorable train of events that would end in her becoming Mrs. Thomas Rowntree. That was exactly what she had wished and what she had planned.

Why, then, that disagreeable feeling of uncertainty?

She pushed it to the back of her mind and went on to complete her negotiations with Gussie, which ended entirely satisfactorily, after which Haggart had to be bearded in *his* den — the stables — and informed of the role he was to play in the escape to Kent. As she had expected, he was scandalised by the whole affair, read her a severe lecture on the total unseemliness of her becoming involved in such a matter, and ended by promising, with a great deal of grumbling and a great many gloomy prognostications, to carry out the part that had been allotted to him in the plan.

Which left Mrs. Lighton to be coped

with, and this turned out, unexpectedly, to be the most difficult part of the business, for, in spite of what Eugenia had referred to as her liking for crests, she was reluctant to allow Muffet to disappear from the London scene just when, as she confided to Eugenia, she was in a fair way to getting her off.

"For you may have noticed, my dear," she said, "that Mr. Blenkinsopp has been growing *most* particular in his attentions, and it never serves to allow a gentleman to cool off in these little affairs. An absence even of a week or two may well be fatal, so much sought after as he is, you know!"

Eugenia, who knew that Muffet had no opinion at all of Mr. Blenkinsopp, a callow youth who had expectations of coming into a very pretty property in Derbyshire but had otherwise absolutely nothing to recommend him to a young female, being much more at home in a cock-pit than in a drawing room, was seized with inspiration and repeated a piece of gossip she had heard from Gussie, to the effect that young Blenkinsopp, having run himself to a standstill in London's more notorious gaming-hells, was about to be sent home to Derbyshire by his outraged papa upon a repairing-lease.

Mrs. Lighton, the first to admit that Lady Chandross's information upon the latest *ton* gossip was more reliable than her own, was visibly chagrined by this news, but, rallying swiftly, said they must concentrate on Mr. Fincher then, who was a widower and a bit old, perhaps, for dear Amelia, but might very possibly be brought up to scratch.

Fortunately, Mr. Fincher had been obliged to leave London at the moment upon business, and was not expected to return for almost a fortnight; so permission was obtained for Muffet to depart from the metropolis as well for a brief visit to her home in Kent. Eugenia and Muffet, in celebration of their success, danced an impromptu waltz together in the upper hall of the slim house in Green Street and then flew to their respective writing-desks, Muffet to indite a brief letter to her mama informing her of their impending arrival, and Eugenia to despatch a somewhat longer but even more mysterious epistle to Lady Brassborough, in which her assistance was requested in a matter of life and death, and the shelter of her roof invoked for "two innocent victims of circumstance."

Meanwhile, the innocent victims of circumstance themselves were put on notice, via a message conveyed by Haggart, to hold themselves in readiness to leave for Kent early on the Monday morning. If they had been having second thoughts as to the wisdom of the plan to which they had agreed, it was not visible in their faces as they emerged from Old Nan's cottage, two striking figures in the claret-and-silver Chandross livery previously procured for them by Haggart, at the cost of a small bribe and a certain amount of prevarication about a joke to be played by Miss Eugenia upon one of her friends. Gerald was grinning and Richard wore his usual composed and impenetrable air; and after a word with Eugenia they took their places up behind and were whirled off through the bright, early-morning sunlight to begin their journey into Kent.

For the first hour of that journey Eugenia had the feeling that the carriage was at least twice as large and conspicuous as it actually was, that everyone they met was looking at them intently, and that it could not have been more obvious to the general public that Gerald and Richard were wanted by Bow Street if they had been wearing large placards proclaiming that fact across their chests. But her heart eventually ceased its erratic jumping each time they approached a turnpike gate, and when they were obliged to halt at an inn to bait the horses she was even able to alight from the carriage with an appearance of entire composure and bear Muffet off to a private parlour to partake of a nuncheon there, while Haggart and the two "footmen" entered the coffeeroom to regale themselves with cold beef and foaming tankards of homebrewed.

The meal was not enlivened by Muffet's nervous conviction that they would walk downstairs at its conclusion to be met by the sight of Gerald and Richard being haled off to gaol by the pair of Bow Street Runners she was quite sure must have followed them from London, and Eugenia was obliged to nip her arm severely in order to prevent her from crying out in alarm when the waiter unexpectedly returned to the room with a fresh pot of coffee.

But to say the truth, as they learned when they did go downstairs to find their twin footmen lounging outside the inn door, exchanging badinage with a pair of grinning ostlers, the greatest danger they had encountered had come from a very dirty and very disreputable old man in a disgraceful old coat, who had been sharp enough and malignant enough to call the attention of the company in the coffeeroom to the marked resemblance they bore to the description of one Gerald Liddiard, wanted for murder and robbery on the King's highway, that had been posted for some time now in the inn.

"Now if 'twas *two* of 'em that was wanted, we'd have 'em both," he had said. "A matched pair, that's what they are," and he had gone off into a long and rheumy chuckle at his own witticism that had ended in his demanding another pint of ale from the landlord.

Gerald had remarked, with a very well counterfeited air of cynicism, that if he had the chance he would change places with Gerald Liddiard any time he said the word, for *he* was a gentleman, the poster said, and it stood to reason he would never see the Nubbing Cheat, but would be got off by his relations and live out his days in happy idleness as a "once-a-month" man on their largesse.

"Ah," he said with conviction, "he can have my place any day, and I'll take his. What about you, Dick?" — grinning over at his "twin."

Richard had replied philosophically that he didn't consider the place a bad one, being as in their last there had been half a dozen children and the nursery on the top floor, which meant you had no sooner finished lugging one can of hot water up three pair of stairs before another was wanted; and the discussion had then wandered off into safer channels.

Haggart, a scandalised onlooker at this bit of byplay, relieved his feelings as the two young men mounted to their places by informing them severely that one of them was as bad as t'other, and if they didn't stop tempting Providence they would soon enough find themselves in the basket.

"Three pair of stairs indeed!" he said to Richard; but Richard only smiled that rare smile of his, and Gerald remarked that if he had known before this how handy it was to have a twin he would have scoured the countryside to find one, as it appeared to him that one could never be taken to account for anything one did as long as one had a double who might just as well have done it himself.

Eugenia was sufficiently cheered by the successful outcome of the journey to this point that she felt her spirits rising, and they improved even more when she began to see, through the carriage window, what was, to her, home country. Huge, honest manor-houses built of massive timbers and rich-coloured Wealden brick; hedges showing a summer tangle of meadowsweet and wild Canterbury bell;

low, square-towered churches; a dreamy disorder of hills, thick woods, and winding lanes — this was the world of her childhood, the world to which she would be able to return when she married Tom.

But at the thought of Tom and her approaching meeting with him, that hollow feeling of uncertainty returned, and it was only by resolutely fixing her mind instead upon their forthcoming arrival at the Dower House, and on the anxious question of whether Lady Brassborough would be willing to receive the two ''innocent victims of circumstance,'' that she was able to be rid of it.

The Dower House — a Jacobean mansion that had served as the principal seat of the Barons Brassborough until the Sixth Baron, prospering in the second George's reign, had erected a larger and more imposing edifice upon a hill a mile or two away — lay well-concealed behind a pair of wrought-iron gates and a magnificent avenue of Spanish chestnuts at the end of the village, some miles to the west of the Manor. As the carriage bowled up the avenue and came to a halt before the south front, with its energetically projecting bays and steep, finialled gables, Eugenia saw the front door open and a magnificent, bulky figure appear dramatically in the aperture. No discreet, soberly garbed butler this, but Lady Brassborough herself, brocaded and bejewelled, all rich greens and purples, like a peacock. She advanced down the steps to the carriage, and as Gerald jumped down to open the carriage door and let down the steps to allow Eugenia and Muffet to emerge, she raised a *face-à-main* to her eyes and regarded first him, and then Richard, fixedly through it.

"Ha!" she ejaculated, in the voice that had thrilled Drury Lane Theatre from pit to gallery when, during the latter years of her reign upon the London stage, just before her marriage to Lord Brassborough, she had begun to play heroines in melodramas instead of saucy breeches parts in rollicking comedies. "What have we here? Not *one* Gerry, but a pair. If you will tell me how to go about dividing oneself into two, dear boy, I shall be eternally grateful. I am sure I have quite enough avoirdupois today for two. And why footmen? Am I to employ you both? I shall be delighted! Eugenia, dear child —'' She enveloped Eugenia in an ample embrace, from which she released her at once to point to Muffet. ''And who is this?'' she demanded.

Muffet, finding herself the cynosure of a pair of magnificent but remarkably worldly-wise and pessimistic dark eyes, which seemed to convey an extreme skepticism as to her being anyone worth knowing, said, trembling, that she was Amelia Rowntree.

''You know the Rowntrees, Lady B.,'' Eugenia said. ''Their land marches with ours — I mean with Coverts.''

''Ah, yes!'' Lady Brassborough continued to fix Muffet with that disparaging gaze. ''Your dear mama does not recognise me, I believe,'' she said, in her deep voice. ''Do *you* recognise me, Miss Rowntree?''

Muffet gave a sort of terrified affirmative squeak, being unable to manage any more coherent reply, and

Eugenia said sensibly, "Of course she recognises you, Lady B., or she wouldn't be here. Could we go inside now, please? And perhaps Gerry and Richard could go upstairs and change into their real clothes at once, so your servants will not think it so queer that you are having them as guests. You *do* realise you are to have them as guests, and that absolutely no one is to know they are here — don't you?" she asked anxiously.

"Do I?" said Lady Brassborough, raising her brows. "Your letter was remarkably unclear, dear child. But if you are giving me two handsome young men all for my very own, I shall forgive you. There are remarkably few handsome young men in this part of Kent. Come along, Gerry."

"That's Richard," Eugenia called after them, as Lady Brassborough took Richard's arm and sailed off into the house with him. She hastened to follow, with Muffet and Gerald. "He is Charles Liddiard's son," she explained. "Did you ever know Cousin Charles, Lady B.?"

"For one brief, glorious moment, when

I was married to poor B.," Lady Brassborough said, without turning round. "I came down to Kent with him — B., that is — and, if memory does not fail me, Charles and I dallied at a hunt breakfast. A charming boy, but fickle — fickle. At least I *believe* his name was Liddiard."

They had entered the hall, all black-and-white lozenge marble floor and pale, faded tapestries, and were met at this point by an extremely ancient butler, who tottered up to receive hats and wraps without demonstrating the least surprise at finding his mistress arm-in-arm with a footman in full livery.

"Matthieu, *mon cher*," Lady Brassborough addressed him in what could only be described as highly Anglicised French, "these are my friends, *les Messieurs* Liddiard, who have come to make me a small visit. No one outside this house is to know they are here — *comprenez-vous?* Now take them upstairs, *s'il vous plaît,* and tell Dunoyer they are to have the Blue Bedchamber and the Green one. *Allez-vous-en!*" she

221

finished, with a dramatic wave of one arm.

The old butler nodded and tottered off up the broad oak staircase, followed by *les Messieurs* Liddiard. Lady Brassborough then led Eugenia and Muffet into a large saloon, which was crowded with such an assortment of excellent French furniture, curios in and out of cabinets, portraits, miniatures, theatrical mementoes, tambourframes, novels, and elegant bonbons that Muffet, who had never seen it before, was confused to the point of attempting to seat herself in a Louis XIV *fauteuil* already occupied by a fat, belligerent pug.

"No, no, not there, my dear!" said Lady Brassborough reprovingly. "That is Wellington's chair. He never allows anyone to sit there but himself." She gathered the pug into her arms, where the resemblance between his pugnacious face and her own appeared to a dazed Muffet almost too close to be true, and, seating herself upon a delicate gilt sofa with a theatrical grace that belied both her bulk and her years, said encouragingly to

Eugenia, "And now, dear child, you must tell me all about your little mystery, and why Gerry has suddenly acquired a twin and become a footman."

"Very well," agreed Eugenia, "only we can't stay long because we are expected at the Manor. But you already know, of course, about the trouble Gerry is in?"

She looked enquiringly at Lady Brassborough, who offered her and Muffet bonbons, told Wellington severely that he was too fat to have one, and selected one for herself.

"Not," she said comfortably, "that I am not too fat, too, but fortunately Wellington cannot tell me that, though I daresay he would dearly like to. Is it the affair of Barnstaple's coachman you are talking of?"

"Yes," said Eugenia, "but he really didn't do it, you see. It was Captain MacGoff; only he was riding Gerry's mare and wearing Gerry's coat, and so Lord Barnstaple told the Authorities that it was Gerry, and naturally they believed him."

She launched into a hurried account of

the matter, including the manner in which Richard Liddiard had been drawn into it. When she had finished, she found that Lady Brassborough was regarding her with no alteration in the expression of experienced skepticism with which she ordinarily faced the world.

"Mad!" she pronounced. "Quite mad, the lot of you. Of course I shall be delighted to help you, dear child, but one does rather see — doesn't one? — that your two young men may be obliged to pay me a somewhat protracted visit if that horrid creature MacGoff isn't turned up. He did me the honour, you know," she said sententiously, "of making me an offer some half dozen years ago — was taken all over queer, I expect, when he set eyes on these" — she held out her magnificently ringed hands — "and felt that the only cure for what ailed him was to make me Mrs. MacGoff at once. I believe I must have been wearing the Pontowski emeralds as well that evening, which of course was quite enough to overset him completely."

"How horrid for you!" said Eugenia

indignantly. "I wonder he dared —"

"Dear child, an offer of marriage is never to be despised when one has more than nine-and-thirty years in one's dish," Lady Brassborough said, "even though it comes from the dustman and is inspired by one's diamonds rather than by the brightness of one's eyes. It is all far more amusing than playing Patience, you see, and reminds one of happier days, when one was rejecting dukes and marquises *ad infinitum,* if that is the term I mean to use — or is it *ad nauseam?* Only I never was, because I always enjoyed it, even when they were quite plain, like poor Aldersworth, or a bit wanting, like old Lord Parradine, who brought me a stuffed llama from Peru, rather like a cat laying a mouse on your doorstep to show how clever she has been, only of course far too large to keep —"

Eugenia, foreseeing that the spate of Lady Brassborough's reminiscences might keep them far too long at the Dower House, necessitating embarrassing explanations at the Manor where there were going to be enough of them due already, at this point said they must take their leave, and shepherded Muffet out to the waiting carriage.

CHAPTER

12

Twenty minutes later the carriage was drawing up before the Manor, a comfortable mansion built in the characteristic Tudor style of half-timbering and the multicolored, winy-blue Wealden brick. Mrs. Rowntree was on the watch for them, as Lady Brassborough had been, and came hurrying out to the hall to greet them the moment the door was opened to them. She was a stout, placid woman, though she did not look very placid at present, having taken the idea firmly in her head, upon receiving Muffet's letter announcing her imminent arrival with Eugenia, that one or both of them had either disgraced herself irretrievably in London or was at death's door.

Of course, upon finding the two of them quite undamaged in either reputation or health, she gave vent to her feelings by loosing a scold upon them, which was interrupted by the entrance of the Squire, who had been out on the Home Farm with his bailiff and was very pleased to see his little Muffet at home again.

"So you've had enough of London already," he said, pinching her cheek. "Well, well, it was your mother's notion to send you there, you know, but I never liked the idea myself above half. 'It's Lombard Street to a China orange,' I said to her, 'that she'll pick up some whipstraw of a park-saunterer there and bring him home to us as our future son-inlaw.' "

"Oh no, Papa!" Muffet said indignantly. "I shall never marry anyone, and certainly not a — a park-saunterer, whatever *that* is. I shall always live here with you and Mama and Tom."

The Squire, who was a large, jovial man, laughed at that and said that might be all very well as long as he and her mother were above ground; but Tom's wife, when he married, might not be quite so pleased to have her in the house, which made Muffet cast a conspiratorial glance at Eugenia and smile. Eugenia, to her own surprised annoyance, felt herself colouring up, and when Tom walked into the room a few minutes later, having been out with his gun after rabbits, she had an odd panicky sort of feeling that she wanted to run away, which Tom had certainly never inspired in her before.

Tom was a tall, fair young man, with a ruddy face and blue eyes that echoed his father's, and it was certain that as the years passed he would grow to be just as stout and jovial as the Squire, and keep his land in good heart, and become the sort of man the whole county could, and only too frequently did, rely on, just as it now relied upon his father. Eugenia, of course, was too young to know all this now, but she did know that Tom was the best friend she had ever had, except for Muffet, and that if she was suddenly feeling with horrid clarity that she did not wish to marry him and never would, it was because there was something wrong with her and not with him.

As a result, she felt a kind of pall of guilt at her own disloyalty hanging over her all during the excellent dinner, featuring a couple of ducklings and a plump leveret, with a soup made of fresh peas and the Savoy cake of which she was particularly fond, to which she presently sat down. And when the Squire retired after dinner to the estate-room and Mrs. Rowntree, seating herself with her embroidery-frame in the large oak-beamed drawing room, suggested that the young people might like to take a turn outside instead of sitting indoors, as it was such a sultry evening, she was hard put to it not to give way to that panicky feeling and say she was tired and going upstairs to her bedchamber, rather than face a conversation *à trois* with Muffet and Tom.

But the conversation, when they had walked outside, began, at least, upon a subject that had nothing to do with the vexing question of her marrying Tom. She and Muffet had agreed beforehand that the best means they had of discovering if Captain MacGoff was in that part of Kent was to take Tom into their confidence and enlist his assistance. He would be able to make enquiries in the neighbourhood without arousing suspicion, and might, at any rate, already have heard of the Captain's presence there.

They were hardly out of the house, therefore, and into the long summer dusk outside, with lightning flickering uneasily over the horizon and a thin moon showing and disappearing behind ominous clouds, before Muffet had embarked eagerly upon the reason for their journey into Kent. Tom listened, spellbound. He had all a healthy young man's taste for adventure, and instantly declared, when he had heard what was wanted of him, that he would not only discover if MacGoff was in the neighbourhood, but would engage himself personally to hand him over to the Authorities.

"Well, I don't think it would be wise for you to do *that*," Eugenia said, "because, of course, he will simply deny that he had anything to do with the matter unless Gerry and Richard can think of a way to make him confess. Gerry says he will choke the truth out of him and Richard says it will be better to try to get it from his groom, who was there when it all happened and may be persuaded to turn King's evidence. But, at any rate, I think you had best leave it to them.''

Tom said rebelliously that he wasn't going to be left out if he knew it, but as he promised to take no action, if he was able to discover MacGoff's whereabouts, without first notifying Gerald and Richard, Eugenia was not seriously concerned about his doing anything rash.

By this time they had wandered round to the kitchen garden behind the house and, having got in among the pea-sticks, were eating the young peas, after their excellent dinner, with unimpaired appetites.

"But, Tom," Muffet, who had got slightly in advance of the other two, called back to them presently, "Eugenia hasn't told you her *other* reason for wishing to come home with me. She has had the most *splendid* idea — at least, I do hope you will think it is splendid, too.''

She turned to look expectantly at Eugenia. Eugenia, finding Tom's enquiring eyes upon her as well, was seized once more with panic, cast a violently reproachful glance at Muffet, and said hastily that they might talk of it another time.

Muffet looked at her in surprise. "But you *said* you would ask him just as soon as you saw him," she said.

"Ask me what?" demanded Tom.

Eugenia, backed into a corner, said desperately that, if he really must know, it was about getting married.

"About getting married?" repeated Tom, puzzled. "About whose getting married? Are you —?"

"Oh, no — *no!*" Eugenia disclaimed hastily. She saw Muffet's astonished eyes upon her and went on, with rather the same feeling, it seemed to her, that she might have had if she had been about to fling herself over a precipice, "That is, not unless *you* want to —"

"Unless *I* want to?" Tom stared at her.

"Unless I want to do what?" Comprehension slowly dawned. "Unless I want to *marry* you?" he demanded, a dumbfounded look upon his face.

Eugenia nodded miserably. How, she wondered, could she ever have thought that it would be easy to ask any man, even Tom, to marry her? And the worst of it was, she felt, that, now she *had* put the matter to him, he would undoubtedly consider he could not, in chivalry, do anything but agree, and she would have to go through the rest of her life with a man (for Tom *was* a man now, she suddenly realised, and not merely a boy she had grown up with) who had married her only out of a sense of obligation.

But here she had reckoned without Tom. For although he had, as if by the touch of a magic wand, suddenly turned into a man before her very eyes, no such necromancy had transformed her, for him, into anything other than the companionable, plucky, sometimes troublesome little girl who had shared in most of his boyhood adventures and escapades. He stared at her severely.

"I think you must have windmills in your head!" he said. "Why the deuce should I wish to marry you — or anyone else, if it comes to that? Oh, I daresay I shall be obliged to some day, to keep up the name; but I shan't be ready even to think of that for years and years and — well, dash it, *years!*"

Eugenia was conscious of a sudden feeling of relief that seemed to flow deliciously from her head down to her very toes; but before she could speak Muffet had flung herself once more into the conversation.

"Oh no, Tom! How *can* you be so cruel?" she cried reproachfully. "Don't you *know* Eugenia will be obliged to accept someone like Mr. Walford or Lord Cazden's son if you won't marry her, and go and live abroad in diplomatic circles or at least in London, and we shall never see her again? And we could all be so *very* comfortable if you only will —"

Tom, who now had the driven, obstinate look of a bull with its horns lowered, quite determined not to be chivvied through a gate, said that was all very well, but why did she have to accept anyone?

"Because," said Muffet, in the voice of a teacher explaining the obvious to a particularly backward pupil, "she hasn't any money! And you *can't* expect her to go on living at Mere forever!"

Tom was heard to mutter mutinously, why not, but at that moment an ominous flicker of lightning in the darkening western sky, followed at once by an emphatic clap of thunder and a sudden determined patter of raindrops upon the pea-sticks, put an abrupt end to the conversation and sent them all pelting off for the house.

By the time they had reached it, the rain was pouring down in good earnest from the angry clouds above, and they entered by the kitchen door, it being the closest at hand. Here they found Cook with two housemaids and the scullerymaid clustered about her, all of them obviously in a state of the highest agitation.

"Ow, Master Tom!" gasped Cook, as she shrank back from the invasion of three breathless and somewhat damp young people into her spotless kitchen. "How you did frighten me, to be sure! Rushing in like that, and me with the palpitations coming on already, what with the storm and having Bow Street Runners in this very house!"

"Bow Street Runners!" The words came from all three of the young people, in accents ranging from incredulous joy (Tom) to sheer horror (Muffet).

Cook, much gratified by the sensation she had caused, said modestly that she couldn't say she had seen them herself, but that Gladys (indicating the elder of the housemaids) had, being as she had been sent for to look for Miss Amelia and Miss Eugenia, who weren't to be found nowhere, though Madam had said they were sure to be just outside, and it seemed they were the ones the Runners wanted to see.

"Oh!" said Muffet in a hollow voice. "We are? I mean, they do? How very — how *very* strange! I wonder what they can want of us!"

She looked imploringly at Eugenia, who had just succeeded in quelling a horrid vision of Gerald and Richard having been run to earth at the Dower House and haled away to Newgate by the comforting thought that the Runners could have no possible reason for interviewing her and Muffet if they had already laid hands on their quarry.

"Yes, it *is* very strange," she said firmly, casting a warning glance at the two young Rowntrees. "I think we had best go and see why we are wanted, don't you? Perhaps it is because we have just travelled down from London, though I can't believe we met any desperate criminals on the way."

"Gladys says as she thinks it's about Mr. Gerald, Miss Eugenia," Cook volunteered helpfully, in the hushed, triumphant voice of one breaking the direst of news; but Eugenia was already leading her two young friends out of the kitchen.

There were voices coming from the drawing room, so she turned her steps directly to that apartment. When she walked in, she at once recognised the two Bow Street men she had seen at Mere

Court on the day that Richard had escaped to London. They were standing just inside the door, looking stubborn and rather grim, while the Squire, who had obviously concluded ringing a peal over them only the moment before, had his back to the cold hearth and looked flushed and furious.

Mrs. Rowntree, her good-natured face puckering into an expression of puzzled distress as she sat looking from her husband to the Runners, was the first to catch sight of the three young people as they entered the room, and she said at once, thankfully, "Oh, here you are at last, my dears! Where in the world can you have got to, with this dreadful storm coming on?"

"That will do, Millie!" said the Squire. He strode across the room and placed himself beside Muffet. "Now, Baker, or whatever your name is," he angrily addressed the taller of the Runners, a capable-looking man of about forty, "here is my daughter, *and* Miss Liddiard, and I'll thank you to repeat to their faces this farrago of accusations you have loosed on me behind their backs!''

Baker, looking obstinately at the Squire from under his thick, greying brows, said he wouldn't exactly say accusations.

''It's only,'' he said, addressing Eugenia, as Muffet had shrunk so far behind the bulwark of her father's stout form that only the tip of her nose and a glimpse of frightened blue eyes were to be seen, ''it's only that we've had information laid, miss, as to two young ladies coming down into Kent today, travelling with a servant who bore a strong resemblance, or so 'twas said, to one Gerald Liddiard, wanted for murder and robbery —''

''Which only goes to *show*,'' Mrs. Rowntree interrupted earnestly, also addressing Eugenia, ''how mistaken they are, my dear, for I am sure Haggart does not in the least resemble poor Gerry, besides being old enough to be his grandfather, or as near it as makes no difference. And, at any rate,'' she went on, regarding the Runners severely, ''you both said there were *two* of them a moment ago, which *proves* that your informant must have been drinking, as no one could possibly wish to travel with *two* coachmen, even if they *did* look exactly like each other.''

'' 'Tweren't coachmen, missus,'' the second Runner, whose name was Cartwright, suddenly said hoarsely. '' 'Twere footmen,'' and he relapsed again into bashful silence.

''Well, that only makes it worse,'' Mrs. Rowntree declared, nothing daunted, ''because it seems those two children were allowed to travel down here quite alone, except for Haggart, with no maid or footman of any sort in attendance, which I cannot help thinking was *quite* remiss of my sister Lighton and Lady Chandross, and so I shall tell them when next I see them. I may be old-fashioned, but in *my* day —''

''Millie!'' said the Squire again, in an awful voice.

Mrs. Rowntree, who was not in the least afraid of her husband, looked vexed, but for the sake of peace in the family subsided.

''You see,'' said the Squire, turning to

Mr. Baker with an obvious air of suffering fools, if not gladly, at least with all the patience at his command, "that my wife corroborates my statement that my daughter and Miss Liddiard arrived at this house today accompanied only by an elderly coachman we have all known for donkey's years as Haggart, and who could not by any stretch of the imagination be Mr. Gerald Liddiard in disguise. Also, to my certain knowledge, Gerald Liddiard has not, nor ever had, a twin brother. He was an only child, as I should think even Bow Street could have discovered by this time if they had put their minds to it."

"We know that, sir," said Mr. Baker, looking harassed. "That's what has us so betwattled. But still Miss *did* tell us, when we went looking for him at Mere Court, that 'tweren't him that had been there, but another man who looked enough like him to be his double —"

He looked over at Eugenia, and in a sort of cold panic she thought, "He is going to ask me directly now, and if I lie he will know it. I must *do* something —"

But to her astonishment — and, indeed,

to the astonishment of the entire company — it was Muffet who stepped into the breach. Muffet moving forward from behind her father's sheltering shoulder and speaking with the calm of desperation with which she had so often faced Miss Bascom when matters had seemed at their blackest for her and for Eugenia.

"If you please, Papa," she said, "Lady Chandross did send two footmen with us. They didn't come to the Manor because their mother was ill at Tunbridge Wells and they wanted very much to visit her, so Eugenia said they might. And Haggart is to take them up again on his way back to London, so that Lady Chandross need never know they did not come all the way with us."

She avoided, with the skill of long experience, the astounded eyes of the Squire and the suspicious ones of the Runners, gazing limpidly instead at a dim portrait of a Rowntree ancestress simpering down upon them demurely from the opposite wall.

Mr. Baker was the first to recover his voice. "And where," he demanded bluntly of the Squire, "is this man Haggart now, sir, if you please?"

The Squire, a good deal thrown off his stride by his daughter's disclosures, gazed at him in some perplexity. "Why," he said slowly after a moment, "he *said* he was going to visit his sister. Yes, that was certainly what he said." The perplexed frown deepened upon his ruddy face. He looked over at his wife. "My dear," he said, "did you ever hear that Haggart had a sister?"

"Of course he hasn't a sister," Mrs. Rowntree said. "'Or if he has, she must be in Scotland. Perhaps that is it — though it *does* appear odd that he should go to Scotland by way of Kent. It all seems very peculiar —"

The Runners looked as if they found it very peculiar as well. Mr. Baker said to Eugenia, regarding her grimly, "And what were the names of these two footmen, miss, if *you* please?"

"Charles," she said promptly. "Charles and James." Everyone had footmen called Charles and James; the names came automatically to her lips.

"Charles and James what?"

She raised her brows in faint hauteur. "Really, I have never troubled to enquire," said Miss Eugenia Liddiard, who knew the full names, family connexions, and domestic problems of every servant who had ever lived beneath the same roof with her.

The Runners, put in their places, looked depressed; then the hoarse-voiced man suddenly began, pronouncing the formula as if hopeful that the familiar sound of it might lead him to some way out of the mental maze in which he seemed to be wandering, "Interfering with a hofficer of the Law in the performance of his dooty —"

"Nonsense!" said the Squire irritably. "No one is interfering with you, my man. My daughter has explained the matter to you very clearly. If you wish to go off to Tunbridge Wells and look for these footmen of the Chandrosses', you may certainly do so and nobody will interfere with you in the least — though why you should take it into your heads to believe that Chandross would hire his own cousin

245

as a footman, and should also happen to have in his employ another footman who could pass as his twin, is beyond *my* understanding."

He looked disgustedly at the Runners, who held a brief, muttered colloquy with each other, of which Eugenia could distinguish only the words "Tunbridge Wells" and "diddled." Quite plainly, they believed themselves to be the victims of some conspiracy, but whom to accuse among the five people confronting them, and of what, they obviously had not the least idea.

There was nothing for it, it appeared, but for them to depart — a rather horrid fate just at that moment, for the heavens had now opened outside and a summer deluge was pouring enthusiastically down, blown by a gusty wind and accompanied by occasional deafening thunderclaps. But neither the Squire nor his lady, although famous in the neighbourhood for their hospitality, took pity upon the hapless minions of the Law, who vanished into the night with upturned coat collars and heads bent against the wind.

"Disgraceful!" said the Squire wrathfully, as the door closed behind them. "Makes a man wonder what the country is coming to, when they send such fellows out to maintain the Law! As if Gerry Liddiard would be clothheaded enough to ride about the countryside perched up upon a travelling chariot for any fool to gape at, when he knows every Law officer in the country is looking for him!"

Muffet, who was feeling rather faint after her heroics, looked at Eugenia, who said purposefully that she was tired and thought they should go upstairs at once to bed.

CHAPTER
13

"So you see," Muffet said rather helplessly as she and Eugenia, in dressing gowns and nightcaps, were at last alone in Muffet's comfortable bedchamber, seated together upon the big fourposter draped with faded flowered worsted damask, "it was the only thing I could think of to say; so I said it. And I did feel so dreadful, having to deceive Papa, but I *couldn't* betray Gerry —"

"No, of course you couldn't," Eugenia said warmly. "I think you did perfectly splendidly — far better than I could have done, for my mind went perfectly blank. Those two Runners may very well go off to Tunbridge Wells now, and that will at least give us time to turn around and think what we are to do —"

A knock fell upon the door.

"That will be Tom, I expect," Muffet said, and slid down off the bed and ran to let him in.

It was indeed Tom who entered the room, looking flushed with excitement and quite undisturbed by the fact that both Muffet and Eugenia were *en déshabillé.*

"I say," he said immediately, "what are we to do now? Had I best ride over to the Dower House, do you think, and warn Gerry that the Runners are on his trail?"

"Goodness, no!" Eugenia said with decision. "For all we know, those Runners may still be lurking somewhere about, waiting to see if we will do exactly that, and lead them straight to Gerry. We had far better go nowhere near the Dower House just now."

Tom, who was obviously burning to do something, looked dissatisfied, and said in that case what *were* they to do?

"Look for Captain MacGoff, of course," said Eugenia promptly. "That is the most important thing. Of course Muffet and I won't be of much use in that, because *we* can't go falling into conversation with people in the taproom of the Swan or enquiring at that horrid little lodging-house in the High Street where he was always used to stay when he wasn't in London. So that will be all in *your* hands, Tom."

She had by this time all but forgotten about the embarrassing incident that had taken place earlier that evening among the pea-sticks, and was somewhat surprised to see that Tom, instead of replying, was gazing with what seemed a kind of bemused attention at her seagreen dressing gown. This elegant garment was trimmed with the same Brussels lace that formed the ruffles of the delicately embroidered nightcap framing her face, from which her silky dark hair now tumbled in loose ringlets down her back. Tom, of course, was quite accustomed to seeing her with her hair down her back — indeed, he had never seen her with it up until she had arrived at the Manor earlier that day — but for some odd reason the sight of those masses of soft dark hair, taken in conjunction with a fetching and fashionable negligee, now seemed suddenly to impede his breathing, and he found his thoughts whirling right away from Will MacGoff and Bow Street Runners and going back instead to the scene among the pea-sticks.

He could not remember exactly what had been said, because it had seemed to him the height of absurdity at the time that little Eugenia Liddiard had been babbling about marriage; but now the scales, as it were, had fallen from his eyes and he saw that she was really not little Eugenia Liddiard at all, but a strange young woman with an enchanting face and a lovely, supple figure, with her elegantly rounded arms emerging from a foam of lace —

"Tom!" Muffet's surprised voice cut through his dazzled reflections. "What in the world is the matter with you? Didn't you hear what Eugenia said?"

Tom pulled himself together and said, more gruffly than was necessary, that of course he had. A kind of exhilaration had begun to replace the dazzle of that moment of revelation, but it would certainly not do to let Muffet see it. His mind began to plan in great satisfying, disconnected leaps how he could find MacGoff, frighten him into a confession, and bring him in triumph to the Runners, thus causing this new Eugenia to regard him with admiration and gratitude. If he could somehow manage in the process to rescue her as well from persecution and danger, life, he felt, would be wholly perfect.

Meanwhile, Eugenia and Muffet, disregarding him, had begun to plan their own activities for the morrow, and had decided to kill two birds with one stone — that is, to lure the Runners away from the Dower House in the event they were still lingering in the neighbourhood and to help Richard prove the legitimacy of his birth — by making a canvass of all the vicarages and rectories in the vicinity in a search for the record of a marriage between Charles Liddiard and Susan Justis. To the Squire and Mrs. Rowntree they would merely have gone out for a long, rambling ride with Tom, but actually the three of them would part soon after they had left the Manor, Tom to pursue his enquiries after Captain MacGoff in the village and Eugenia and Muffet to make their own investigations among the ecclesiastical records of the various churches in the neighbourhood.

"So that if the Runners decide to follow *us*," Eugenia said, "instead of going off to Tunbridge Wells to look for Gerry there, they will be wasting their time, and Gerry and Richard will be quite safe at the Dower House. I wish we might warn them that there are Runners down here looking for them, but I expect it isn't worth the risk, and I *do* think they will be sensible enough not to show themselves in the neighbourhood."

So Tom, dismissed from Muffet's bedchamber, went to his own to plan suitable heroics for the following day, which fortunately dawned clear and bright after the evening's storm, so that no objection was voiced by Mrs. Rowntree to the expedition the young people had planned. Eugenia, in a fashionable blue riding-dress and a hat with a jaunty little feather that quite completed Tom's dazzlement, parted from the other two at the foot of the lane that led to the highroad, and in a few minutes was galloping down a chalky lane bordered with speedwell and thrift in the direction of the villages that lay to the east of the Manor.

It had not occurred to her, when she had formed her plan, that the making of enquiries concerning a marriage that might or might not have taken place between Charles Liddiard and Susan Justis more than a quarter of a century before could be not only fruitless — she had been prepared for that — but also fraught with considerable embarrassment. The name of Liddiard was well-known in the neighbourhood, and even the most reverend of gentlemen, she soon discovered, was apt to be quite unable to contain his curiosity as to the reason for her interest in his ecclesiastical records. Unfailingly polite and helpful these gentlemen indubitably were — so polite, in fact, that she was obliged to share the family luncheon of cold beef and rice pudding at one rectory and to endure what amounted to a guided tour of the Church of St. Faith conducted by its vicar, who insisted upon her admiring the three large table tombs with their knightly effigies resting eternally under beautiful, crocketed, ogee-headed canopies: admirable examples, as he enthusiastically informed her, of the workmanship of the late Decorated period of the mid-fourteenth century.

But all these clerical gentlemen were also obviously bursting to know why Miss Eugenia Liddiard should be, so to speak, quartering the county like a game dog, searching for evidence of a marriage between a long-dead cousin and a young woman with whose name none of them was familiar. It had been a quarter of a century now since the Justises had disappeared from Kent, and not one of the reverend gentlemen Eugenia met that day had been the incumbent in his particular parish for that long a period of time. All any of them could tell her was that there was no record of Charles Liddiard's having married anyone at all in his own particular church, and it was accordingly a disappointed Eugenia who kept her rendezvous with Muffet and Tom at the foot of the lane leading to the Manor that afternoon.

Her spirits were dampened the more by the reports given by Muffet and Tom of their day's efforts. Muffet's enquiries had drawn the same blank as had her own, while Tom's had been only slightly more successful. He had heard, it was true, from two separate sources that MacGoff had recently been seen in the neighbourhood, but neither of his informants had been able to tell him where the elusive captain was staying. For all Tom knew, he might already have left Kent again, for he had last been observed driving a smart curricle, with his groom up behind, along the road leading to Tunbridge Wells.

"Well, we shall simply be obliged to try again tomorrow," Eugenia said, endeavoring to keep up their spirits and her own; but it soon developed that even that might be somewhat difficult to do, for when they returned to the Manor they found Mrs. Rowntree in something of a pucker over their protracted absence and full of the matter of a social engagement to which she had committed them during it.

"A young man named Walford called while you were out," she was in haste to tell them, "such a very agreeable young man, my dears! — and said he had made your acquaintance in London and, hearing from Lady Chandross that you were both come down to Kent upon a short visit, as he was just about to go upon a visit to an uncle of his in the neighbourhood as well, he said he ventured to ride over this morning and enquire if you would attend a strawberry-party his uncle was giving tomorrow — Oh, I have not told you. He — the uncle, that is, to be sure — is Mr. Childrey, the rector of St. Aldwyn's. Of course I have heard of him for time out of mind, and how it has come about that I have never met him I cannot think, only that we have never had a great deal to do with that part of the county except when my poor mama was alive, for her sister Lizzie lived in Dymchurch for a great many years, you know —"

By this time Mrs. Rowntree had entangled herself so inextricably in the meanderings of her own words that she was obliged to halt and consider where she had got to.

"Of course," she went on brightly after a moment, "I told him you would be delighted to accept his kind invitation," and looked in some surprise at the three gloomy faces before her. "My dears," she said reprovingly, to Eugenia and Muffet, "I know you must be fagged to death with all your London gaieties, but, really, it would have been *quite* uncivil to refuse, when Mr. Walford had ridden all the way over here on purpose to invite you! And it will not be in the least like a London ball, you know — only a few people, and the weather so delightful —"

Eugenia and Muffet, resigning themselves to the inevitable, said of course they would go, and had a few exasperated words with each other later on the subject of well-meaning parents. Still, they told each other, they could each visit another rectory in the morning, before Mr. Walford's uncle's odious strawberry-party had to be attended, and Eugenia said philosophically that at any rate the Runners, if they were still in the neighbourhood, must be thoroughly mystified by their peregrinations, and were probably convinced by this time that Gerry must have sought sanctuary in a church, as criminals had done in the Middle Ages.

So on the following day, after another fruitless morning excursion, Eugenia arrayed herself in a charming frock of rose-pink cambric with double scallop work around the hem, and Muffet donned a somewhat less modish but very becoming one of sprig muslin, and, each having provided herself with a broad-brimmed gypsy hat against the sun, they were borne off from the Manor in the Rowntrees' old-fashioned carriage. Tom, who had absolutely refused to accompany them, though he had most kindly, his mother informed him, been included in the invitation, had the intention of continuing in pursuit of Captain MacGoff, so that the afternoon, at any rate, was not to be entirely lost.

The rectory in which Mr. Walford's uncle, Mr. Childrey, had been placidly pursuing the even tenor of his ways for close to forty years stood at the western end of one of those Kentish villages in which time appeared to have stopped several hundred years before. Half-timbered houses smothered in summer flowers and greenery, an ancient inn with minute windows peeping from beneath its deep, dark thatch, ducks sedately afloat on a small stream under a tiny bridge — all lay shining in summer sunlight and enfolded by the slow green sweep of the downs.

The rectory itself was a drowsy-looking, red brick house set behind a low brick wall and wrought-iron gates, with enough of its original glebeland left to it that its garden, bounded by a row of tall, clipped limes, sloped down to the stream, with an embanking wall topped by a flat stone parapet from which one could agreeably observe the incredibly peaceful flow of the green-shaded water below.

Young Mr. Walford, on the watch for

them, led them into the house, which was quite as serene within as it was without, all shining old wood and faded Chinese wallpaper, and introduced them to the rector. Mr. Childrey was a tall, thin, courteous gentleman with silvery hair, who looked as if he must have been chosen for his post because his peaceful, elderly house needed a peaceful, elderly clergyman to complete its perfection; but actually he had been a young and rather dashing bachelor when he had first come to St. Aldwyn's, and it had taken him all of forty years to attain his present suitability.

"How do you do, my dear?" he said to Eugenia, as he took her hands gently in his. "I knew your father, you know. Such a handsome young man! Of course that was many, many years ago. And so you and Perry are to —"

"No, no, Uncle!" Mr. Walford's strangled, horrified voice interrupted him. Eugenia, seeing at once that Mr. Childrey, to whom, as to many absentminded people, past, present, and future are as one, had leapt to the conclusion that what he had no doubt heard discussed as a possibility for the future was already a *fait accompli,* almost had the giggles, and Mr. Walford went on babbling incoherently, rapidly introducing several unrelated subjects into the conversation, all of which had the virtue of having no connexion whatever with a projected marriage between himself and Miss Eugenia Liddiard.

On this flood of words he got her and Muffet out of the house and his uncle's presence, leading them to join a small group of ladies and gentlemen who were already wandering through the well-tended strawberry-beds and regaling themselves with the sun-warmed fruit. There was, Mr. Walford babbled on, to be a cold collation set out in the dining room, as it was such a very warm day, though it had originally been the plan to pic-nic under the limes, but in the meanwhile would they care to taste the strawberries?

Eugenia, with her usual excellent appetite, said they most certainly would, and, having been provided with a small basket and an introduction to the other ladies and gentlemen, was soon absorbed into the party and would have enjoyed herself thoroughly if she had been able to free her mind from its nagging worry about Richard and Gerald.

Ought one of them, she wondered, she or Tom or Muffet, cease being so very cautious and ride over there to the Dower House to see how matters were progressing there? After all, the Runners had apparently vanished from the neighbourhood; nothing had been seen or heard of them since they had gone out into the storm that evening from the Manor. Most probably they were in Tunbridge Wells now, searching for a pair of elusive twin footmen; perhaps they had even gone to London. She really must, she felt, have some word soon with the two young men and reassure them that the search for MacGoff was being diligently pursued, or one or both of them might grow impatient and be led into doing something rash.

A voice at her elbow suddenly interrupted her thoughts.

"Miss Liddiard?" It was young Mr. Walford, very pink in countenance, either as a result of picking strawberries in the hot sun or from some inward disturbance of mind. "May I — may I have a word with you?" he enquired, his face now emulating a whole sunset as he brought out the request. "It is — it is perhaps a little cooler — there —"

He indicated the low parapet overlooking the little stream at the end of the garden. Eugenia looked at him, her initial surprise giving way to interest.

"Good gracious, I do believe he means to make me an offer!" she thought, quite without either the triumph or the perturbation that a well-brought-up young lady ought to have felt under the circumstances. "How very odd he does look, to be sure!"

She wondered if she ought to tell him at once that she really did not wish to marry him and put him out of the mental agony that was now turning his suffused countenance almost purple; but that hardly seemed feasible, since he had not as yet asked her and there were several people in the vicinity who would infallibly overhear every word she said. So she followed him docilely down the garden to the parapet, seated herself upon it, and waited kindly for him to speak.

Nothing happened. Had she been able to read his mind, she would have known that young Mr. Walford was frenziedly debating within himself whether he ought to: a) sit down on the parapet beside her; b) cast himself immediately upon his knees before her; or c) remain upon his feet and launch, in the dignified manner of a Member of Parliament rising in debate before his colleagues, into his subject.

As she was not gifted with any such esoteric powers of divination, however, she merely wondered why in the world he did not get on with it, and meanwhile leaned over to watch with interest a goggle-eyed fish steer himself through the clear brown water and rise just in time to seize an unwary fly that had descended dangerously close to the surface. It was very warm and still in this part of the garden, with the voices of the other guests coming distantly through the sun-filled air and the water flowing gently by below, the only movement in this enchanted landscape. A Sleeping Beauty sort of landscape, Eugenia, not ordinarily given to poetic fancies, found herself thinking; only poor Mr. Walford was certainly not the Prince to awaken one. She leaned over — the wall was low, the little stream very close, and she could just trail her hand in the gentle brown water.

"Oh, Miss Liddiard!" said Mr. Walford suddenly, galvanised into speech by the romantic sight of a young lady in a remarkably pretty frock and a broad-brimmed hat tied with pink ribbons trailing her hand in a very picturesque stream; and he put his whole soul into the words. "Oh, Miss Liddiard!"

Eugenia looked up at him enquiringly. The next moment, to her entire surprise, for she had certainly not expected anything so romantic from young Mr. Walford, he had got down on both knees before her and was fervently clasping her hands in his.

"Oh, Miss Liddiard!" he pronounced again, as if intoxicated by the sound of her name. "Eugenia!" (that, it seemed, was even better.) "Will you be mine? Will you be my wife?" And then he spoiled everything by adding conscientiously, "I have Lord Chandross's permission to pay my addresses to you —"

Eugenia, who had surprised herself the moment before by experiencing an odd, almost terrifying, but certainly exhilarating sensation somewhere inside her — was it because in the sun-dazzle, the shifting dapple of leaves on his form, it was almost possible to imagine that it was not Mr. Walford, but someone else, someone hidden behind all that golden shimmer of light, who was speaking those words to her? — came back to reality at the sound of Lord Chandross's name and said practically that Lord Chandross really had nothing to do with it.

"He'd say I could marry anyone, so long as he wasn't too disgraceful a person to have at Mere," she said. "Do get up, Perry. Of course we shall always be very good friends, but I couldn't marry you."

"Why not?" demanded Mr. Walford, stung into practicality himself by this kind but exceedingly firm refusal. He got up and brushed off the knees of his fawn-coloured breeches. "*I* think we should deal extremely well."

Eugenia said, still kindly but with the slightest hint of impatience, no, they wouldn't.

"I don't see why not," Mr. Walford argued, though perhaps with a feeling on his own side that she might just possibly be right, for a young lady who could receive one's offer of marriage so very coolly was certainly not what one had been thinking of when one had gazed spellbound at the picture she had presented a few moments before in her rose-pink frock and wide-brimmed hat. "There isn't anyone else — is there?" he enquired, with sudden jealous suspicion.

Eugenia began to say scornfully, of course not, and then stopped. The words died on her lips, and as she sat gazing at Mr. Walford his sturdy form seemed to melt and dissolve in the sun-dazzle and she was looking at someone else — a tall figure, a bronzed face with heavy-lidded black eyes beneath strongly marked brows. "Oh, *now* I know!" everything inside her seemed to rise to tell her, with a certainty that took her breath away; and Perry Walford, gazing at her, thought that her eyes were like stars and, forgetting her misconduct of a few moments ago, asked her to marry him all over again.

"No, Perry, I can't. Really I can't," Eugenia said, but more kindly now, although in an odd, distrait way, it seemed to him.

She turned away from him again and looked down at the water. Mr. Walford, feeling that he had been dismissed, swallowed once or twice, tried without success to say something more, and after a few moments went disconsolately away. Eugenia continued to sit gazing at the water. A pair of ducks paddled sedately by, and the sun went behind a large white cloud for a moment and then came out again as brightly as before. She had the feeling of being in a dream in which the familiar landscape of her life had suddenly become a place into which she had never ventured before and in which magical possibilities and griefs lay on every side. Griefs because of course

Richard did not love her and no doubt considered her only as a rather tiresome girl who had meddled in his life with disastrous results; but one could not have everything. What one had was the joy of knowing love.

A voice spoke beside her, interrupting her thoughts just as Perry Walford's had interrupted them a short time before.

"My dear Miss Liddiard, sitting here all alone? This will not do." It was Mr. Childrey. He sat down beside her, smiling his gentle, absent smile at her. "We are all about to go into the house now and have some *real* food," he said to her. "Sun-warmed strawberries are all very well, but hardly sustaining fare, I fear. I hope you are enjoying yourself?" he enquired a trifle anxiously.

Eugenia said she was enjoying herself very much, and then, her mind still full of Richard, was beginning to consider if she had best take advantage now of being at St. Aldwyn's to enquire of Mr. Childrey whether a marriage had ever been performed there between Charles Liddiard and Susan Justis, when the

Rector startled her by himself saying in a mild, reminiscent tone, "I married your father and your mother, you know. Dear, dear, how many years ago that was, and what a very handsome pair they were! I thought with no little pleasure, I assure you, when Perry introduced me to you this afternoon, what felicitous fruit that union had borne —"

He broke off, seeing that Eugenia was gazing at him with a perfectly dumbfounded expression upon her face.

"But — but —" she stammered after a moment, "you *couldn't* have! Married Papa and Mama, that is. They were married in London, at St. George's, Hanover Square. Oh, Mr. Childrey, tell me quickly — are you *quite* sure it wasn't *Charles* Liddiard you married, and not *Walter?*"

Mr. Childrey, looking a good deal perplexed by this sudden, urgent appeal, coming upon him so unexpectedly out of the drowsy, sun-filled afternoon, appeared to consider the matter.

"Dear me," he said after a moment, "I really cannot say, my dear child. I took it for granted, of course, when Perry first mentioned your name, that you were the daughter of the Mr. Liddiard who owned Coverts —"

"Yes, I am!" Eugenia said earnestly. "But you really *couldn't* have married *him,* Mr. Childrey, so it must have been some other Liddiard. *Could* it have been his cousin Charles, do you think? He was married twenty-six years ago, and we think it was somewhere in Kent — but it will all be in the church records, won't it? Oh, Mr. Childrey, *could* we go and see?"

She had jumped up and stood before him, her face imploring and vivid with excitement. Mr. Childrey looked more perplexed than ever.

"To be sure," he said. "My wretched memory — I really do not recall whether the young man's name was Charles or Walter, my dear. We shall certainly look at the register presently, if you like — but, as you see, I cannot desert my guests just at this moment."

He had risen too now, and was offering her his arm to escort her back to the house; there was nothing for it but for her to accompany him, and then to sit through what was, to her, an interminable period, sipping orgeat and nibbling at the excellent cakes and aspics and sandwiches that were offered her, but which might have been made of sawdust, for all she knew. Her mind was seething with mingled dread and jubilation — dread that the marriage of a gentleman named Liddiard at St. Aldwyn's might be nothing but a figment of Mr. Childrey's erratic memory, jubilation over the possibility that she might soon be able to present proof of his legitimacy to Richard and, with that proof, the ownership of Coverts.

At the other side of the room Perry Walford, who seemed to be taking her rejection of his suit with some understandable sulkiness, was being solaced by Muffet, to whom he had blurted out the whole story, and who, as a heroine-worshipper of Eugenia herself, was quite ready to sympathise with his feelings. They really would make an excellent pair, Eugenia thought, observing the manner in which Muffet's blue eyes rested consolingly and yet somehow hopefully upon her companion's face, and, with the wish of a new lover to push everyone else into his or her own state, she formed a resolution, in the tiny corner of her mind that was not already preoccupied with greater concerns, to do everything in her power to see to it that young Mr. Walford had every opportunity to pursue his latent interest in that direction.

At last the moment she had been waiting for arrived: the final guest had taken his departure, and Mr. Childrey, his duties as host now accomplished, was free to institute a search through the records of a quarter century past for the name of Charles Liddiard.

"I remember it all *quite* well, you see — only not the name, the Christian name, that is," he told a breathlessly expectant Eugenia as his thin hands turned the dusty pages of the register in which Kentish couples who were now grandparents had hopefully inscribed their names. "Such a splendid-looking young woman, only in a state of some agitation, it seemed — not that that was not quite normal under the circumstances — a special licence, a runaway match, one could not but suspect. Still, everything was quite regular, so that one could not refuse to perform the ceremony — Ah, here we are!"

His thin finger pointed to a pair of faded signatures — one bold and dashing, the other painstaking and tremulous — upon the brittle page. *Charles Frederick Norrys Liddiard. Susan Elizabeth Justis.*

"Exactly so!" said Mr. Childrey triumphantly. "I knew I could not be mistaken." He turned to Eugenia solicitously, observing her brimming eyes. "But, my dear child, you are not crying?"

"Oh yes, I am!" said Eugenia, horrified by her own weakness, but too filled with exultant joy at her discovery to care. "But it is only because I am so happy! Oh, Mr. Childrey, you *will* take very good care of that book — won't you? Because, you see, such a great, great deal depends upon it!"

CHAPTER
14

In the same golden late-afternoon heat that enveloped the rectory of St. Aldwyn's, the Dower House drowsed to the hum of bees and the rustle of a faint breeze in the Spanish chestnuts. Upstairs in her bedchamber Lady Brassborough, who had concocted a plan of her own which she had not as yet communicated to her two guests, having but a poor opinion of the discretion of young men, was being assisted by Hortense, her ancient dresser, into a toilette that was warranted to astound all beholders, consisting of a crimson brocade gown, a turban of crimson satin shot with gold and embellished with a plume of curled ostrich feathers, a tinsel shawl, spangled Spanish slippers, and the Pontowski emeralds, which mounted her majestic bosom in heavy splendour to fall in an unbelievable cascade to her nonexistent waist. Her magnificent dark eyes were alight with mischief, and her wide, mobile mouth had put off skepticism for the moment and was slightly primmed in an expression of satisfaction.

In the large saloon below, Richard Liddiard, bored with elegant confinement, turned the pages of a novel and thought of a long, exhilarating gallop over the downs. He had just won several thousand pounds from Gerald at picquet — a purely academic debt, however, as both were penniless and had not the slightest expectation of receiving funds from any source. Gerald, even more bored with life than was Richard, had said he was going upstairs to his bedchamber and sleep until it was time for dinner, but instead he had wandered out of the house.

Most unwisely, it seemed. It was difficult to imagine, in the golden somnolence of these bucolic surroundings, that danger might be lurking among the Spanish chestnuts or crouching behind the rhododendrons; but, even as Gerald strolled aimlessly along the terrace, it was soon to appear that eyes were upon him. Once, twice, he traversed its length, and if he had not been half asleep while he walked, filled with a daze of summer warmth and silence and boredom, he would no doubt have noted the stealthy waving of a bush that no vagrant breeze had set in motion, and glimpsed the shadow of a figure slipping noiselessly, when his back was turned, from one point of cover to another.

Mr. Baker, of Bow Street, was famous — though of this Gerald was happily unaware — for the Pounce with which he frequently captured his unwary victims.

Gerald reached the end of the terrace and turned again. The sun was now directly in his eyes; he half closed them, squinting against its golden flood of brilliance, and on the instant was seized from behind by a powerful grip.

"Got him!" said Mr. Baker's voice in a grunt of satisfaction.

He held on grimly as Gerald, gathering his bemused senses to a realisation of the attack, twisted violently in his grasp in an attempt to free himself; but the effort was in vain. A second figure had already sprung from those suspiciously waving bushes and Mr. Cartwright, coming nimbly to his colleague's assistance, had in a moment reached their prey from behind and pinned his arms firmly to his sides.

"Got him!" he repeated Mr. Baker's words, while Mr. Baker, drawing a pair of manacles from his pocket, clapped them dexterously upon Gerald's wrists.

"In the name of the Law, I arrest you, Gerald Liddiard, for the wilful murder of Josiah Slook!" said Mr. Baker, panting slightly from his exertions. "And a good job, too!" he added, in justifiable self-congratulation.

Gerald, very pale, was beginning upon a furious but somewhat inarticulate protest when his voice was suddenly suspended. He was gazing at the front door of the Dower House, and the two Runners, glancing up sharply to see what it was that had engaged his attention, found themselves staring at what was apparently the double of the man they now held in their clutches. The apparition, who still held an elegantly bound novel in one hand, with a finger between the leaves to mark the place where he had given over reading, advanced towards the group on the terrace in a leisurely manner.

"My dear boy," he said to Gerald, raising black brows over what seemed to the two astonished Runners a pair of remarkably quelling, heavy-lidded eyes, "what is this? Some jest, I imagine? But in rather poor taste, it would appear to me."

The two Runners, each still grasping one of Gerald's arms, gazed at each other in open dismay. Quite obviously they were furiously debating within themselves the question of whether they ought to release their present captive and seize this new arrival upon the scene; but as the new arrival showed no signs of wishing to escape from them, and on the contrary appeared to have every intention of remaining where he was, they came to a mutual determination to retain the bird in the hand rather than endeavour to capture the one in the bush and maintained their hold upon Gerald.

Gerald himself, who had perceived in a moment the game that Richard meant to play, prudently remained silent, leaving it to the Runners to make the next move.

It was Mr. Baker who spoke. "And who might you be, sir?" he enquired cautiously of Richard, standing ready, as it were, to act upon information received.

The strongly marked black brows went up again.

"Do you know," drawled Richard, "I believe I might far more properly put that question to you — as well as demanding why you have seen fit to clap a pair of manacles upon a gentleman who is a guest in this house. I have no doubt that Lady Brassborough will be most seriously disturbed by such an occurrence —"

Mr. Baker, looking somewhat abashed but still determined, said they were Bow Street Runners and had a lawful warrant for the arrest of one Gerald Liddiard.

"One Gerald Liddiard," Richard repeated thoughtfully. "*One* Gerald Liddiard. Are there two, then?"

Mr. Baker and Mr. Cartwright looked at each other, baffled.

"Not two *Gerald* Liddiards, in course," Mr. Baker said then, surrendering to the obvious, but still with bulldog determination. "But one of you two gentlemen is him, and which of you it is I mean to find out."

"Well, you won't find out from me," Richard said. "And as you haven't a *pair* of warrants on you, I suggest you had best let this gentleman go until you make certain which of us it is that you want. And, by the bye, you know, the fact is that you really don't want either of us. That murder was committed not by Gerald Liddiard, but by one — and I do mean *one* — Captain Will MacGoff, riding Gerald Liddiard's mare and wearing Gerald Liddiard's coat. Owing to those circumstances, Lord Barnstaple's identification was somewhat at fault."

But this red herring — for so the Runners appeared to consider it — did nothing to turn them from their intention of arresting Gerald Liddiard. Mr. Baker, with an air of patent disbelief, said that was all very well, but their warrant said Gerald Liddiard, not Will MacGoff, and Gerald Liddiard it was that they intended to have, if they had to obtain the identification from Lady Brassborough herself.

"By all means, then, ask her," Richard said placidly. "I doubt very much that she will be happy to receive you, and I doubt even more that she will be able to tell you which of us is Gerald Liddiard, but by all means put the question to her, if you must. I should advise you, though, to remove those unpleasant-looking manacles from this gentleman's wrists before you go inside. Lady Brassborough is a remarkably broad-minded woman, but even she is not likely to take kindly to the sight of one of her guests in this condition."

But this was something that Mr. Baker could by no means be prevailed upon to do. He had succeeded in placing at least one possible Gerald Liddiard *hors de combat,* and, taking into consideration the size and muscularity of the other, he had no inclination to place himself and his colleague at what was certain to be a disadvantage if his prisoner were free to use his fists as well.

So Gerald, to his deep annoyance, was obliged to enter the Dower House in his manacled state under the unblinking and incurious eyes of Matthieu, the ancient butler, who had lived so long and seen so many things that he would have shown an equal lack of surprise if the Prince Regent had been ushered in in a similar state between a pair of warders.

"Priez Madame la baronne, s'il vous plaît, a venir ici," said Gerald, who had learned that Matthieu would respond to his very bad French far better than to the most painstakingly uttered English.

Matthieu said, *"Oui, monsieur,"* and obligingly moved towards the staircase; but at that moment Lady Brassborough herself, in all the startling splendour of crimson brocade, ostrich plumes, and enormous emeralds, appeared at its head and peered down upon the strange little assemblage below.

"Hortense! *Hortense!*" she called her dresser in stentorian tones. The ancient little dresser scuttled into view. "Bring me," commanded Lady Brassborough, "my *face-à-main*. My eyes, it seems, are not what they were. Is that young man in manacles, Hortense?"

"*Oui, madame,*" confirmed the dresser, squinting down at the group below.

"Im-possible!" said Lady Brassborough, in the tones she had employed in her memorable farewell performance, when she had essayed, for the first and only time in her career, the role of Lady Macbeth. She began to descend the stairs in a slow and menacing manner. Mr. Baker and Mr. Cartwright visibly quailed, and Richard looked appreciative and amused. Decidedly, there was no need to fear that Lady Brassborough would not take her cue and give a performance calculated to render the greatest possible benefit to her two young guests in the way of confusing and daunting the unwelcome Runners. "What," she enquired, when she had accomplished the stair-descending performance with maximum effect and had placed herself directly before the now highly flushed Mr. Baker, "what, if I may enquire, is the meaning of this, my good man?"

Richard and Gerald remaining maliciously silent, Mr. Baker was obliged to answer the question himself.

"If you please, my lady —" he began, in an unhappy voice.

"Wait!" commanded Lady Brassborough. She held up one hand in a dramatic gesture. The little dresser, scuttling down the stairs to her, handed her her *face-à-main,* which Lady Brassborough raised to her magnificent dark eyes, surveying Mr. Baker and his colleague through it with merciless intentness. She then slowly lowered it and said in an even more imperious tone, "Continue!"

Mr. Baker swallowed; his Adam's apple jumped convulsively.

"Yes, my lady," he said obediently.

"Well, you see, my lady, it was like this. In the execution of our dooty, we apprehended a cove — a gentleman — we take to be Gerald Liddiard, wanted for murder and highway robbery —"

"You have the wrong man," Lady Brassborough said instantly.

"The wrong man?" Mr. Baker's eyes leapt triumphantly to Richard's face; he took an involuntary step in his direction.

"The wrong man," Lady Brassborough repeated severely. "The man you should have arrested in this matter, my good idiot, is Captain Will MacGoff. He will be arriving here shortly, and you may then proceed to the execution of your dooty, as you call it, and arrest him."

"Arriving here!" The exclamation came simultaneously from Richard and Gerald, and Gerald at once continued, in a tone of incredulous jubilation, "Do you mean to say you've found him then, Lady B.? By God, you *are* a Trojan!"

"Of course I have found him," said Lady Brassborough complacently. "It was not at all difficult. I merely allowed the notion to get about that I had heard he was in the neighbourhood and that I was pining to see him again, and of course he has taken the bait, the silly juggins! We have exchanged billets-doux, and he will be here within the half hour."

Precisely how she had "allowed the notion to get about" she did not say; it might have been presumed to present some difficulties, as there had been no visitors to the Dower House since her two young guests had arrived there, nor had she herself gone out; but then there are always deliveries made, and butchers' boys can carry a tale through a village as rapidly and efficiently as a fire runs through a tinder-dry forest.

At any rate, neither Richard nor Gerald was inclined to enquire into her methods at the moment, while the Runners, much confused by the turn events were taking, stood consulting each other with their eyes and wishing in a somewhat cowardly way that they had not been clever enough to capture Gerald Liddiard after all, since in the first place it appeared that it would take the wisdom of a Solomon to discover if he really *was* Gerald Liddiard, and in the second place, it might not be Gerald Liddiard they wanted in the first place.

"Meanwhile," Lady Brassborough was saying to Mr. Baker in her imperious voice, "you may remove those repellent gyves from this gentleman's wrists, and then we shall all go and sit down and make our plans. I do think we ought to have a plan, so much simpler in the long run, though if one leaves things to themselves they often sort themselves out in the most extraordinary way. Do get on with it now, my good man!" she added with some severity, as Mr. Baker merely stood staring at her in a bemused fashion. "MacGoff will be here very shortly!"

Mr. Baker, recognising the voice of authority, gave it up and unlocked the manacles.

"Good!" said Lady Brassborough. "And now come along."

She led the way into the saloon, where Mr. Cartwright, quite bewildered by its grandeur of crimson and gold, tried to take Wellington's chair when invited to sit down, and was rewarded by being bitten, though fortunately, as he was wearing buckskins, not through to the flesh.

"And now," said Lady Brassborough, gathering the indignant Wellington into her arms and seating herself in a large *fauteuil* like an empress upon her throne, "to business. I take it that you two gentlemen" — she turned upon Messrs. Baker and Cartwright the brilliant, mischievous dark eyes with which Meg Morvin had lured the hearts from the breasts of their fathers in the gallery of Drury Lane Theatre a generation ago, and they at once fell down, metaphorically speaking, at her feet — "I take it that you are interested in apprehending the man who shot Lord Barnstaple's coachman on the Bath Road in the course of a highway robbery. But first, you see, we must have proper evidence that he did it, which is why I am about to form a plan. I have had a great many ideas on the subject, because when one has acted in as many plays as I have, plots are really six for a penny, so to speak. But it seems to me that the best, now that you are most providentially here as representatives of the Law, would be the one in *The*

Deceiver Deceived. Are you familiar with the piece? No? Then I shall tell you all about it."

And her ladyship, to the intense bewilderment of her auditors, proceeded to unfold for them a highly complicated story of intrigue in high life, the salient point of which appeared to be the concealment of various persons, *solus* and in groups, behind a large screen, whence they popped out at inconvenient moments upon the other players as they engaged in clandestine activities, most of them having to do with the tender passion.

"Of course, no one is in love with anyone *here*," Lady Brassborough said, looking from one to the other of the Runners rather accusingly, they felt, as if convicting them of derelection of duty upon this point, "though I daresay MacGoff may pretend to be, as he may not quite have given over hope of prevailing upon me to marry him. But the point is that we *do* have the screen" — and she pointed triumphantly towards a very large Chinese one, full of polite mandarins and sloe-eyed ladies — "and so you may all hide behind it while I lure MacGoff into a damaging admission. I am very good at luring," said her ladyship with some pride, "though I must say I have never attempted it in a criminal case before this time. And then you may pop out at the proper moment and arrest him 'in the execution of your dooty', as you say, and not trouble Gerald any longer."

The Runners again gazed at each other in helpless dismay. It was obvious that they understood little of the "plan" that Lady Brassborough had unfolded to them, and, indeed, neither was quite sure at the moment that he was not being dragooned into taking part in some sort of theatrical performance, staged for purposes of her own by the gorgeously eccentric lady seated opposite them.

But all thought of revolt against the very peculiar program that was being drawn up for them was put out of the question the next moment by the sound of a jaunty *rat-tat-tat* abruptly sounding upon the knocker of the front door.

"There he is now!" exclaimed Lady

Brassborough, springing to her feet with an agility that belied her age and bulk. "Quick, quick, all of you — behind the screen!"

The two Runners, to their intense discomfiture, found themselves being herded, as if by a large and energetic sheep dog, behind the tall Chinese screen, where they were rapidly joined, in rather close quarters, by Gerald and Richard.

"And not a sound, mind you," Lady Brassborough admonished them, "or you will spoil everything. Wellington, my darling, no, no, no!" These last words were addressed to the pug, who, apparently feeling that the unfortunate Mr. Cartwright was attempting to escape without suitable chastisement for his act of trespass, was engaged in a vigorous attack upon his boots, accompanied by furious growls. "This nice man is going to be a great help to us," said Lady Brassborough, gathering Wellington up reprovingly, "so you must *not* bite him. You may bite Captain MacGoff, if you like, because he — Oh, here he is now!" She looked up, beaming, as a tall, coarse-looking, powerfully built man of about forty, in a coat of vaguely military cut, strode into the saloon, putting aside the protesting Matthieu, who was vainly endeavoring to announce him in a properly formal manner. "Will MacGoff," she said, looking up into his broadly grinning face, "I have just been telling Wellington that he may bite you if he likes, because it has been such ages since you have been to see me! And now sit down and tell me everything you have been doing, you naughty, naughty man!"

She seated herself invitingly upon a crimson satin *tête-à-tête*.

The Captain, who was regarding the fabulous flow of emeralds over her ample crimson brocade facade with cupidity gleaming brightly in his rather small eyes, promptly seated himself beside her.

CHAPTER

15

To the four eavesdroppers crowded together behind the Chinese screen, the half hour that followed was, to say the least, an extraordinary and somewhat unnerving experience. Few men have been privileged to be observers — or at least auditors, for none of them could see over or around the screen — of a courting scene between a fullblooded military gentleman of uncertain respectability and a lady of ripe years, vast experience, and quite uninhibited manners. An initial embarrassment was the first reaction all around: the two Runners stared woodenly straight before them, earnestly refraining from meeting each other's eyes; Gerald grinned uncomfortably; and Richard looked more than ordinarily detached.

But human nature is human nature, and as the Captain grew more ardent and the lady more coy, four pairs of ears gradually liberated themselves from gentlemanly scruples about eavesdropping upon private conversations and concentrated with an unabashed interest upon that scene of small scuffles, knuckle-rapping fans, and occasional heavy breathing (the Captain) and full-throated chuckles (Lady Brassborough) coming tantalisingly to them from beyond the screen.

"No, no, *no,* you bold, wicked creature!" That was Lady Brassborough: Meg Morvin's famous alto tones, full of laughter and what Mr. Baker and Mr. Cartwright, reading behind the negatives, correctly characterised to themselves as "come-hither." "You forgot yourself, sir! I have promised nothing!"

"Ah, but your letter, most dear lady — your lovely letter!" That was the Captain, naturally, in ardently cajoling Irish. "I have it here!" — and there was a muffled thump, indicating, no doubt, the Captain's attack upon that part of his robust anatomy, probably his chest, where the missive in question was to be understood to lie hidden. "Didn't you ask me to come round here yourself, and didn't you say it might be to my advantage? And didn't you say, moreover, that it might be to *your* advantage as well? Tell me then, what could be more to both of our advantages than the two of us getting riveted? You'll have a fine, strong, handsome husband, and I'll have a fine armful for a cold night —"

Here a sharp, but scarcely violent slap and the sound of a satisfied guffaw reached the ears of the fascinated eavesdroppers, and the Captain's voice said, "Ah, it's a woman of spirit you are, Lady B.!"

"I am," came Lady Brassborough's voice, with more than a little of Meg Morvin's lilting Irish in it in return. "And it's a *man* of spirit I'd be wedding, Will MacGoff, not some poor creature with no more life in him than to be sitting tame by the fire, without so much as a lark or a jolly prank in him! Ah, my poor Brassborough, now — *there* was a roaring boy for you! Many a time we set Paris by the ears, the two of us, before these cruel wars came on — yes, and Lisbon and Vienna, too, if it comes to that —"

"And couldn't we do it again, the two of *us*?" demanded the Captain — "for it's to the Continent I'd be taking you, m'dear, as soon as we'd be wed. I've had enough of England, if you'd know the truth — it's no place for a man of my talents. Listen, now, listen." The Captain's voice became low and urgent. "I've the loan of a yacht from a friend of mine — a decent boat, crew and all — and she's to take me to Antwerp on the Friday. Say the word and we go together. We can be married the moment we set foot on land —"

"Dear boy, you are going far too fast!" Lady Brassborough's voice, accompanied by a series of short, furious barks from Wellington, who apparently shared in this opinion. The Captain swore. "Shocking!" said Lady Brassborough, reprovingly. "Before ladies, or at least *one* lady — for

I *am* a lady, you know, by courtesy of poor Brassborough.''

"The brute bit me," the Captain muttered sulkily.

"Did he?" said Lady Brassborough comfortably. "The dear dog has more sense than a Christian. Of course he doesn't care for you flying at me in that alarming way, as if you were about to eat me up! Here — have my handkerchief."

And then there was the sound, for the four enthralled eavesdroppers behind the screen, of a great clashing of emeralds and a sort of whalelike upheaval on the *tête-à-tête*, which meant that Lady Brassborough was hunting amongst her draperies and appurtenances for her reticule.

"Now," she went on presently, "that is much, much better, isn't it? Such a tiny scratch to be making such a to-do over, and you a soldier! Were you never wounded, then, in all the grand battles you were in?"

This, as Gerald, at least, who was well-acquainted with the Captain, knew, was good for a round quarter hour of highly

299

coloured description of several perfectly apocryphal feats of valour performed by that gentleman in the course of his military career; and he groaned in spirit at the thought of being obliged to remain cooped up in their airless covert on this very hot afternoon while the Captain's reminiscences ran their course. Mr. Baker and Mr. Cartwright had obviously indulged liberally in onions during their midday meal; Richard's elbow was in the small of his back; and he was obliged to stifle a ferocious and persistent desire to sneeze, brought on, no doubt, by the knowledge that it would be quite fatal to all their plans for him to do so.

"God bless Lady Brassborough!" he thought gratefully, as the determined dowager cut ruthlessly into her military wooer's imaginative reminiscences and said that was all very well, but that had been in his grasstime, when he had been young and full of juice, and she had no doubt that what he liked best to do now was to sit by the fire and tell lies about his former exploits.

"Now Brassborough, the dear

creature," she said, "never lost his *élan,* if you have the least idea what *that* means. Do you know what he did just the year before he died, when we were in St. Petersburg? — God knows why, I mean why we were in Petersburg, for it was as cold as hell would be if they turned the temperature in the other direction down there. Well, it happened that he sat down to play with one of those Russian princes — *not* Pontowski, and you may keep your greedy eyes off my emeralds! — and there was some bobbery with the cards. Nothing that Brassborough could prove, mind you, but he was determined to have his money back. So the next time his Russian friend was foolish enough to travel by night he lay in wait for him and held him up, mask and all, like an English highwayman, and took enough from him to make up his losses —"

Behind the screen Gerald and Richard had stiffened to attention at this audacious plagiarism of the Captain's own activities upon the Bath Road. If the Captain, they thought, would rise to the bait — !

The Captain rose.

"By the powers, and didn't I do the same thing myself not a month back," he said boastfully, "when that sneaksby Barnstaple fuzzed the cards on me in a friendly game? Tried to put the change on me, the blackguard, but no man has contrived to do that yet to Will MacGoff! I caught him out on the Bath Road — mask and pistols, just as you say — and had my fair dues of him."

"Barnstaple? On the Bath Road?" Lady Brassborough's voice sounded perfectly calm but not averse to being impressed. "So it was you who was behind that business! But you went Brassborough one better there, I think. Wasn't there a man killed in that little affair? You're a dangerous man, Will MacGoff!"

The Captain said complacently that he believed he was. "A fellow gets used to a little blood," he said, "when he's been in as many battles as *I've* seen, m'dear. Of course, I'd no intention of going so far in *that* business — not the same as war, or the field of honour, you know! If that clumsy fool of a coachman hadn't

302

frightened my horse — sheerest accident that the gun went off, you see! Not that I haven't blown a hole through my man more than once at twenty paces on Paddington Green — ah, it's no milksop you'll be marrying, my love, and you can make up your mind to *that!*"

But the Captain's boasts were allowed to proceed no further. Mr. Baker and Mr. Cartwright had heard enough for their purpose, and the former, stepping out from behind the screen, his pistol drawn and at the ready, announced his identity in emphatic tones and commanded the Captain to stay where he was, as he was under arrest.

The Captain, not unreasonably startled by this sudden irruption of a Bow Street Runner into the scene of his prospering amours, turned pale and swore, but, being a prudent man despite all his braggadocio, remained where he was on the *tête-à-tête* beside Lady Brassborough. He then turned even paler as Gerald and Richard emerged from behind the screen, stared at Gerald, stared even harder at Richard, and finally, recovering himself with a visible effort, managed to say in a blustering tone to Mr. Baker, "Put that pistol up, man! What the devil d'you mean by it, breaking into a lady's drawing room and flourishing firearms about like that? Is it drunk you are then, or mad?"

"Oh no, he isn't drunk — *or* mad," Lady Brassborough said, rising from the *tête-à-tête* as composedly as if she were quite accustomed to having her guests taken in charge at pistol-point every day in the week. "And he hasn't broken into my drawing room, either. I put him behind that screen myself so that he could hear what you have just said to me. You are a great fool, Will MacGoff. You have just hanged yourself with your own long tongue — although I daresay you won't be after all, in the end," she added thoughtfully, "because I have always found that men of your stamp have as many lives as a c-a-t. I don't wish to say the word itself because Wellington holds them all in the greatest aversion and seems to know when one mentions them, even in French, though elementary

304

spelling, it appears, is quite beyond him."

All action had perforce ceased during this interesting monologue, although Gerald was obviously bursting to give MacGoff a piece of his mind over the double-dealing that had made him a fugitive from the Law during the past weeks, and Mr. Baker was equally anxious to pronounce his official formula over his captive. As it happened, however, neither was able to unburden himself even after Lady Brassborough had finished speaking, for at that moment the sound of another voice intruded rudely into the conversation.

"Stand fast, culls!" said the voice, speaking from outside one of the long windows which gave on the terrace, and which now stood open in the late afternoon warmth. "And drop that pistol, or I'll blow a hole through the lady!" This last remark, obviously, was addressed to Mr. Baker, who, like the other occupants of the room, was staring as if bemused at a heavy-set young man in a broad-brimmed, greasy hat and a stained and frayed coat, standing just outside the window with a very serviceable-looking pistol levelled at the group inside. "Drop it, I said!" repeated the unwelcome new arrival, emphasising his words this time by letting off the pistol with deafening effect.

The ball shattered an elaborate lamp just at Lady Brassborough's elbow, and Mr. Baker prudently dropped the pistol.

"Good work, Joe!" said Captain MacGoff, his broad face now creased in an approving grin. "Damme, I was right, you see — it *was* a trap." He moved swiftly to pick up the pistol that Mr. Baker had dropped and dexterously removed a similar one from Mr. Cartwright's coat pocket. "Come inside now and keep these people quiet while I collect the jewels," he ordered the young man called Joe, whom Gerald knew well as the Captain's groom. The young man did as he was bidden, and MacGoff grinned unpleasantly into Lady Brassborough's indignant face. "If I can't have you and your fortune, m'dear," he said, "it seems I must make do with all those pretty baubles you've collected.

We'll start with the emeralds, and those great diamonds on your fingers — I can put them to good use, you see, keeping myself in comfort on the Continent, out of the way of these meddlesome Redbreasts. And then I'll thank you to hand over the key of your jewel-box —''

Lady Brassborough drew herself up to her not inconsiderable height.

''I shall do nothing of the sort —'' she began awfully; but Richard's quiet voice interrupted her.

''You had best do as he says, Lady Brassborough,'' he said. ''He means to have them, you know. This was his real reason for coming here this afternoon, I fancy.''

''Well, you've the right of it there, whoever you are,'' the Captain agreed. ''Not Gerry Liddiard — that's plain to be seen, no matter how much you look like him, for he never said such a sensible thing in his life.''

''You curst blackguard!'' said Gerald angrily. ''You've been clever enough up to this time, haven't you? — but you needn't think you'll get clear with *this* haul. Good

307

God, man, don't you know the house is full of servants? They must have heard that shot, and ten to one some of them have already gone for help!"

"Ay, and by the time they've fetched it, I'll be long gone," the Captain said confidently, "for they're all close on ninety and move like tortoises. Now, Lady B.," he addressed his fulminating hostess, "will you give those emeralds to me or will I take them off you myself?"

Lady Brassborough, casting a glance of ineffable loathing upon him, removed the emeralds from around her neck and dropped them into his outstretched hand.

"Why don't you *do* something, you great looby?" she demanded meanwhile of the helpless Mr. Baker. "I suppose *this* is what one pays rates for — to be robbed of one's valuables in broad daylight, with a pair of Bow Street Runners looking on! *Don't* be in such a hurry!"

This last admonition was addressed to Captain MacGoff, who, after hastily dropping the emeralds into his coat pocket, had seized upon her reticule and was engaged in pawing through it in search of her keys. She pulled the reticule from him and in doing so spilled its entire contents out upon the floor in a mad confusion of scent bottles, handkerchiefs, embroidery silks, scissors, a vinaigrette, and other assorted odds and ends.

The Captain swore and got down on his knees to commence his pawing again, during which diversion Lady Brassborough took advantage of her opportunity and instantly removed several of the large diamond rings she wore upon her fingers and popped them into her mouth.

Unfortunately, this manoeuvre was observed by the greasy youth with the pistol, who promptly informed the Captain of it, and as Lady Brassborough found it impossible to reply in suitably scathing terms to the Captain's order that she remove them immediately without complying with this demand, and on the whole considered it more unsatisfactory to be deprived of speech than of her jewels at that moment, she did so, emitting at the same time a series of uncomplimentary remarks upon the

Captain's ancestry and personal characteristics that made even Mr. Baker and Mr. Cartwright stare at her in respectful admiration.

The Captain, however, remained impervious, dropped the diamonds into his coat pocket to join the emeralds, and, having extracted a set of keys from the magpie contents of the reticule upon the floor, enquired which of them would open her jewel-case.

"I shan't tell you, you rag-mannered, beef-witted, pudding-hearted jackanapes," said Lady Brassborough roundly. "Find it out for yourself."

The Captain said he would do so and, striding over to the door, opened it, revealing a cluster of Lady Brassborough's ancient retainers standing outside, gabbling excitedly in French. They scattered in terror before him as he made for the stairs, brandishing Mr. Baker's pistol, and in the confusion he did not observe that at the centre of the cluster there had been a young lady in a modish frock of rose pink cambric and a broad-brimmed gypsy hat — in short,

Miss Eugenia Liddiard.

Her presence in the hall at that crucial moment had come about as a result of the decision she and Muffet had arrived at to stop at the Dower House on the way back to the Manor from the strawberry-party, for the purpose of allowing Eugenia to acquaint Richard with the good news she had learned at the Rectory. The carriage, in pursuance of this plan, had just drawn up before the front door when its occupants had been startled by the sound of the shot the greasy youth had let off in Lady Brassborough's saloon.

The coachman, a prudent man, had immediately attempted to whip up his horses and remove himself and his passengers from the vicinity; Muffet, alarm had done nothing to stop him; and only Eugenia's threat to jump out of the carriage if he did not stop had obliged him to bring his horses once more to a halt.

Eugenia had then said firmly that she was going inside, had, in spite of the impassioned entreaties of Muffet and the coachman, descended from the carriage, and had mounted the steps and immediately been admitted, even before she had had an opportunity to knock, by the agitated Matthieu. What had happened to Muffet and the carriage after that she had no idea, for she had instantly been engulfed by a group of terrified servants, none of them having the least notion what to do, all of them speaking in animated French, and all anxious to shift the burden of responsibility for action upon the shoulders of a member of the English Quality, even a young female one, who would presumably be more familiar than were they as to the proper method of coping with these extraordinary events.

By the time the Captain emerged from the saloon, Eugenia had managed to gather from the torrents of French descending upon her from all sides that one of the two young men staying with Lady Brassborough had been escorted into the house in manacles by two odd-looking strangers — *"hommes sans importance,"* in Matthieu's disparaging phrase — and that the whole party, plus Lady Brassborough and the other young man, had then gone into the saloon, where they had been joined after a time by Captain MacGoff. As to who had been firing at whom, or why, they had not the least notion, but Matthieu, upon hearing the shot, had fetched from his own quarters a very large and ornate French pistol with a burnished barrel inlaid with silver, obviously far predating the Revolution, which he displayed for Eugenia's edification as soon as the Captain had vanished up the stairs.

"Is that loaded?" she enquired, looking at it skeptically.

"Mais oui, mademoiselle — oui!" Matthieu assured her enthusiastically.

Eugenia, still looking skeptical, investigated the ancient firearm, which appeared to her almost certain to misfire, or, worse still, explode if one attempted to let it off. But she could hear the Captain tramping furiously about upstairs in his search for the jewel-case, and decided that if she was to do anything in the way of rescuing her friends in the saloon she had best do it quickly.

She took a deep breath, walked to the door of the saloon, and flung it open, holding the heavy pistol pointed as steadily as she could straight before her.

What happened next occurred so swiftly that no one was able afterwards to state the precise order of events. The greasy youth, seeing the door open and a young lady appear suddenly upon the threshold with a pistol in her hand, rapidly raised his own weapon; Lady Brassborough uttered a blood-curdling shriek; Richard shouted, "Eugenia — *no!*" and launched himself in a flying leap across the room, knocking the pistol from the greasy youth's hand; the pistol went off, the ball striking the crystal chandelier overhead and sending glass flying in all directions to the accompaniment of a prolonged and cheerful bell-like tinkling; the two Runners flung themselves upon the greasy youth; Wellington bit Mr. Cartwright; and Lady Brassborough fainted into an astonished Gerald's arms.

There was, of course, no doubt whatever as to the outcome of the contest between the two Runners and the greasy youth, once the pistol had been knocked from the latter's hand, and in a matter of moments he was wearing the manacles that had lately been removed from Gerald's wrists and had been pushed down firmly into one of Lady Brassborough's elegant *fauteuils,* with Mr. Cartwright standing over him.

Meanwhile, Richard, aware that the Captain must have heard the shot from upstairs, tore the ancient pistol ruthlessly from Eugenia's hand and, pushing her behind the *tête-à-tête* on which Lady Brassborough and the Captain had conducted their amours, instructed her in a voice that brooked no contradiction to get down behind it. He then moved rapidly towards the door, accompanied by Mr. Baker, who had possessed himself of the greasy youth's pistol, while Gerald, immobilised by Lady Brassborough, endeavoured to deposit her limp and ponderous form upon a sofa in a seemly manner, which was not an easy task, as he was quite unable to lift her and was more or less obliged to drag her into position.

By the time Richard and Mr. Baker had arrived at the door of the saloon the Captain's footsteps were already to be heard rushing down the stairs. He reached the ground-floor hall just as they did and, casting one horrified glance at them, fled precipitately across the hall and shot out the front door, scattering Lady Brassborough's ancient servants, all squawking with terror like a hen-house full of chickens invaded by a fox, right and left as he did so.

Mr. Baker, unable to fire his pistol for fear of injuring one of the servants, made haste to pursue him, with Richard beside him and outstripping him as they ran down the steps; but they were too late. The Captain had already jumped into his curricle, which stood before the front door, and, snatching the reins from the hands of the ancient groom in attendance upon it, whipped up his horses and was off down the drive in a swirl of flying hooves. A ball from Mr. Baker's pistol whistled harmlessly past his ear as he disappeared. Mr. Baker swore.

"Here — you!" he addressed the groom urgently. "I'll need a horse —"

"*Mais non — non!*" old Matthieu's cracked voice came proudly behind him. *"Monsieur verra — tout s'arrangera."*

Richard turned. The old man had come outside behind them and now spoke another sentence in French to Richard, who raised his brows, grinned, and asked incredulously, *"Assurément?"*

"Assurément, monsieur," said Matthieu, nodding emphatically.

"What's he gabbling about?" demanded Mr. Baker hurriedly. "Look here, I need a horse —"

The sound of a loud crash and the frightened neighing of horses came faintly to their ears from down the drive.

"It's all right," said Richard. He clapped old Matthieu cordially on the shoulder. "He says we are not to disarrange ourselves, because he gave instructions to the groom to do something fruitful to the wheels of the Captain's curricle. I should think they — or at least one of them — had just come off. Shall we go and see?"

CHAPTER
16

The peace of a warm, golden, late
summer afternoon had once more
descended upon the Dower House. Mr.
Baker, having rescued the dazed and
bruised Captain MacGoff from the
wreckage of his curricle, had departed
with him, Mr. Cartwright, and the greasy
youth, with profuse apologies to Gerald
and to Lady Brassborough for any
inconvenience he and his colleague might
have caused them. Lady Brassborough,
recovered from her swoon and with her
jewels restored to her, was seated on the
sofa upon which Gerald had placed her,
sipping French cognac, which restorative
to the nerves she had also offered to her

guests, and casting bitter aspersions upon herself for having been weak-minded enough to faint away during the most exciting crisis of the afternoon.

"It is *most* dispiriting," she said. "I have never been so foolish before, even when Brassborough and I were attacked by three armed men in a gondola in Venice, and I pushed one of them into the canal while he ran his sword through the other two."

Gerald said it must have been even more exciting than their little turn-up that afternoon, and then he and Richard, who were both bursting with gratitude towards her for having lured the Captain into confessing his guilt, confounded themselves in praises of her, so that she quite forgot to be depressed over her sad want of conduct in swooning away just as events had become — in her words — really interesting.

Meanwhile, Eugenia, who had also taken, upon Lady Brassborough's insistence, a small glass of cognac as a restorative, was bursting with her own wish to cap Richard's satisfaction at being free at last of the menace of the Law by telling him of the proof of the marriage of Charles Liddiard and Susan Justis that she had obtained at the Rectory of St. Aldwyn's that afternoon. But before she could find a moment's intermission in the conversation in which to make her announcement, there was the sound of galloping hooves outside, followed by a violent attack upon the knocker and an immediate hubbub in the hall.

Lady Brassborough's brows went up. "What now?" she enquired resignedly. "I hope it is not those tiresome Runners coming back to say they have lost their prisoners and we must find them for them all over again."

But it was not Mr. Baker and Mr. Cartwright who burst into the saloon, but, to the astonishment of Lady Brassborough and her guests, a party consisting of Squire Rowntree, Tom, and the Rowntrees' coachman, all armed with fowling-pieces and apparently in the expectation of being required to make instant use of them. At the spectacle of

Lady Brassborough seated calmly upon a sofa, however, sipping cognac, with Richard, Gerald, and Eugenia arranged equally at their ease around her, the Squire, who was leading the party, halted abruptly upon the threshold, blinking.

"But — but —" he stammered. His face suddenly coloured up beetroot red; he turned furiously upon his coachman. "You damned jobbernoll!" he said. "If you've brought us here on a fool's errand —!"

Eugenia jumped up. "Oh!" she said, enlightened. "The shot! You have come to rescue us! How very kind of you, Squire! But you are too late — I mean, it is all over now and we are really *quite* safe."

Lady Brassborough heaved herself up from her sofa and advanced upon the bewildered and now highly embarrassed-looking intruders.

"Mr. Rowntree — isn't it? And young Master Tom," she said, flashing her famous smile upon them. "Won't you sit down — first, of course, allowing Matthieu to relieve you of those alarming-looking firearms — and take some refreshment? Such a *very* warm day, is it not? Matthieu will see that your man has a tankard of ale in the kitchen, and" — she addressed the ancient butler, who was hovering agitatedly in the background — "the Manzanilla, I believe, for the gentlemen, Matthieu. A really excellent sherry —"

She halted, seeing that the Squire was not attending to her, but was staring instead at Gerald and Richard, who had risen and stood together, the former grinning cheerfully at him and the latter regarding him with his usual air of reserved composure.

"Good heavens!" said the Squire in a disbelieving voice. "There *are* a pair of you, just as those damned Runners said!"

"Yes, there are," Eugenia hastened to explain. "Richard is Charles Liddiard's son, you see; and I have found out only this afternoon that Cousin Charles really *did* marry Susan Justis — that is, Richard's mother — because Mr. Childrey, at St. Aldwyn's, says he performed the ceremony himself." She turned to Richard, who had suddenly grown rather pale and stood regarding her with a slight, almost incredulous frown upon his face. "No, it is true!" she protested. "I am acquainted with Perry Walford, who is Mr. Childrey's nephew, and he is visiting at the Rectory and rode over to invite Muffet and me to a strawberry-party there this afternoon, and while I was there I asked Mr. Childrey if he had married Charles Liddiard and Susan Justis, and he said he had. Muffet and I have been making enquiries of all the clergymen in the neighbourhood, you see, but none of them knew anything about Cousin Charles until I asked Mr. Childrey, and he remembered it distinctly, and showed me the register with the signatures in it. It is all *quite* legal, and so you *are* Richard Liddiard and will be able to have Coverts instead of Cousin Cedric," she finished, rather out of breath from talking so fast, for the words had all but tumbled over one another in her eagerness to get them out, while at the same time she rather wished that she had not had to say them before so many people, but had been able instead to tell him quietly somewhere alone.

But there was no help for it now, and she was pleased when the Squire, who had been following her words with great interest, stepped forward and shook Richard cordially by the hand.

"Well, well," he said, "so you are Charles Liddiard's son! I knew your father well, you know; we were just of an age — boys together and all that. Now I daresay you'll be taking up residence at Coverts shortly, and a very good thing for the place that will be! There's Cedric living in Canterbury — never did care tuppence for the land — but when Walter was alive he had a very pretty little stud over there —"

"*Do* sit down, Mr. Rowntree," Lady Brassborough said, firmly interrupting the Squire, who, once in the saddle over county matters and with a clear field before him, might have gone on forever if someone had not taken him hand in hand. "You and Richard may talk horses and land as much as you like then, but we have all had a *very* fatiguing afternoon and I do think we ought to have all these explanations while we are sitting down."

But to everyone's surprise the Squire, thus brought up short, greeted the suggestion with a frown, shot a glance at Gerald, coloured up very pink, and said gruffly after a moment, "No, my lady, I thank you. I *won't* sit down. Not with a man in the room who is under a charge of murder —"

"But he isn't!" Eugenia said, flinging herself once more into the breach. "You mean Gerry, of course, but that is all over now, and the Runners have taken the man who really did it in charge here this very afternoon. That was what the shooting was about, you see. It was Captain MacGoff, and Lady Brassborough very cleverly lured him here and entrapped him into confessing, and he tried to steal her jewels, and then the Runners arrested him. So Gerry is quite cleared now of any suspicion —"

The Squire, who had been attending to this speech in obvious astonishment, exclaimed suitably and at some length, at its conclusion, over this unexpected turn of events, after which he apologised handsomely to Gerald and at last accepted Lady Brassborough's invitation to sit down and partake of the sherry that Matthieu had brought in.

The whole party then settled into a delightful gossip *cum* explanations on the events of the day, with the Squire, Gerald, and Lady Brassborough leading the conversation. Eugenia's own cognac-induced loquacity had by this time deserted her; she was conscious that Richard was sitting quite silent, frowningly regarding the glass of cognac he held in his hand and looking not at all elated by the sudden reversal in his fortunes that the day's events had brought about, and this puzzled and disturbed her. Of course, she thought, feeling somewhat hurt in spite of herself, one did not look for thanks for something that, after all, one had only stumbled upon by the sheerest accident; but she could not help feeling that she had behaved rather well that afternoon, even though Lady Brassborough *had* said that she would rather lose every jewel she possessed than be obliged to go through that moment again when Eugenia had appeared in the

326

doorway with a pistol in her hand and the greasy youth had raised his own pistol to fire at her.

Perhaps, she thought, Richard was vexed with her because she had spoken so openly of the question of his legitimacy before the Squire and Tom; but it was not in the least like him to stand upon his dignity, and he must certainly realise, at any rate, that the tale of Charles Liddiard and Susan Justis was already well known in this district. She sat regarding him rather anxiously, and wishing very much that she might be able to speak to him alone, until presently the sound of carriage wheels upon the drive outside again intruded upon the conversation. A few moments later Matthieu appeared in the doorway to proclaim, with proud satisfaction in at last having a proper visitor to announce, "Miladi Chandross!"

Eugenia jumped. She had not had the slightest notion that Lady Chandross was in the neighbourhood; but even as her ladyship trod into the room, apparelled, as always, in the highest kick of fashion in a modish pomona-green travelling costume and a dazzling bonnet with an upstanding poke-front, the whole sequence of events that must have accounted for her unexpected appearance in Lady Brassborough's saloon at this moment formed itself in her mind. There was not the least doubt but that Mr. Baker and Mr. Cartwright, during the period when they had disappeared from the neighbourhood, had gone, not to Tunbridge Wells, but to London, to question the Chandrosses about the elusive twin footmen who had accompanied the Chandross carriage into Kent; and Lady Chandross, understandably puzzled and alarmed by the incomprehensible appearance of two quite unknown footmen upon the scene, had hastened down to Kent to discover the truth of the matter.

Nothing less than her expectation, Eugenia was dismally aware, that she, Eugenia, might be irretrievably compromising herself by jauntering about Kent in the company of two members of the male sex who certainly were not in the Chandrosses' employ could have induced her to make such a journey, and she looked forward with some apprehension to the explanations that must now inevitably ensue. Her only dependance lay in the hope that the successful outcome of her efforts at clearing Gerald's name would cause Lady Chandross to overlook the reprehensible fact that she had deceived her completely as to her reason for coming into Kent.

But Lady Chandross, though she was undoubtedly, by the coolness of her manner and the unwonted sparkle in her grey eyes, very angry indeed, was above everything a Lady of Fashion, and as such had no intention of descending to bandying words with her ward before strangers. She greeted Lady Brassborough in her usual bored, husky voice, apologised for breaking in upon her, and excused herself upon the grounds that, having just arrived at the Manor, she had been given somewhat alarming news by Mrs. Rowntree concerning the situation at the Dower House as disclosed by Muffet, and had accordingly felt it best to come and see for herself what was going forward there.

Lady Brassborough, who was by this time enjoying herself immensely, what with people coming and going in her house as freely as if it had been a busy posting-house and with opportunities to meddle in other people's business on all sides, said she was to think nothing of it, gave her a glass of sherry, and launched into a vivacious explanation of the events of the afternoon, all of which was accepted by Lady Chandross with her usual air of fashionable indifference. Even the sight of what was apparently two Gerald Liddiards, and the information that one of them was actually Charles Liddiard's legitimate son and, as such, the owner of Coverts, failed to elicit more than a lift of the eyebrows from her; she told Gerald he was a wretch to have set them all by the ears with this latest scrape he had fallen into, but said Cecil would no doubt be so relieved that he, Gerald, was not to be obliged to stand his trial for murder that he might be cozened into doing something handsome for him if he promised to lead an exemplary life in future.

"So it seems that everything has turned out for the best in the end, quite in the manner of one of those dull little comedies where everyone reforms or is suitably paired off just before the curtain falls," she said, shrugging her shoulders as she looked over at Tom. "Eugenia has told me of your plans, of course, dear boy," she remarked to him. "I do hope the wedding will be soon. Long engagements are so dreary — don't you find?"

The Squire stared at her. "Long engagements!" he exclaimed in astonishment, while Tom's face flushed up all over and Eugenia, wishing that the floor might open and swallow her, sat too petrified with shock to say a word. "Why, what do you mean, my lady?" His eyes went accusingly and delightedly to Tom. "Here, you young rascal, what have you been up to behind my back?" he demanded. "Made her an offer, have you? — and without so much as a by-your-leave to me?"

Now, thought Eugenia in miserable expectation, *now* she was about to suffer for her misdeeds. Tom would deny that he had done anything of the sort; the Squire would be upset and displeased; and Gussie — with every right in the world, she was obliged to admit — would be angrier with her than she had ever been before.

But as she waited for the axe to fall, she heard Tom say, astoundingly, "J-just so, sir. I *do* wish to marry Eugenia." She looked over at him in consternation: his face was still highly flushed, but he was speaking quite steadily, and her first swift thought that he had had too much of Lady Brassborough's sherry was obviously doing him an injustice. "If you don't object —" he added, with a rather sheepish glance at his father.

"Object? Not a bit of it! Delighted, my boy! Perfectly delighted!" said the Squire, his broad, cheerful face giving every evidence that he was speaking the truth. "Best thing in the world you could possibly do — settle down early in life with a fine young woman, set up your nursery as soon as may be — no better stock in the county than the Liddiards, you know — no, nor any prettier girl than Miss Eugenia,'' he added, suddenly becoming alarmingly gallant, and putting down his glass to come over and envelop Eugenia in a large, hearty embrace. He then kissed her and said, much to the admiration of those of his auditors who were not too thunderstruck by the turn events had taken to listen, that Tom was a lucky dog and if he was twenty years younger and not already riveted he would have a try at cutting him out himself.

By this time Eugenia had no idea where to look. It seemed quite impossible, so rapidly had the matter developed, to say at this point that they were all mistaken, and that Tom had neither asked her to marry him nor, indeed, wished to do so, that he was acting, in fact, out of a sense of chivalry to protect her from the consequences of the deception she had practised upon Lady Chandross. She and Tom were being felicitated now on every side — by Lady Brassborough, by Gerald, even, she noticed with a sinking of the heart, very civilly and properly by Richard — and she felt that she could not embarrass Tom at this juncture by telling him publicly that she really did not wish to marry him, after all, and that his sacrificial gesture had thus been in vain. Far better to wait until they were back at the Manor, when a more private explanation might be managed.

Gussie, of course, would be furious, but that, after all, did not matter. Feeling as she did about Richard, Eugenia thought, she could not possibly go back to London now and allow Gussie to entice or dragoon some eligible young man into making her an offer.

"I shall simply have to go out as a governess," she thought, hoping for Tom's sake that she did not look as forlorn as she felt.

But Tom was in no case to notice how she looked, being too covered with confusion at all the attention he was receiving to think of anyone but himself.

The party from the Manor, including Lady Chandross, who had accepted Mrs. Rowntree's hospitable invitation to be her guest there while she remained in Kent, now rose to take their leave. Eugenia found Richard taking her hand and thanking her, in a cool, expressionless way that could not have been disapproved of even by Lady Chandross (who had obviously not forgiven him for having taken her in at Mere and then compounding the injury by being actually related to her in the most respectable way), for having turned up Mr. Childrey and the register at St. Aldwyn's.

"Oh, it was nothing!" said Miss Eugenia Liddiard in her most grown-up voice, feeling quite unable to find the proper words to express her own gratitude to this suddenly remote Richard for his having saved her life by deflecting the bullet the greasy youth had meant for her.

And then Lady Chandross called to her to come along, and they all went outside, where the Rowntrees' carriage was waiting, the coachman, relieved to escape from a barbarous kitchen in which only the French language was spoken, already upon the box and ready to transport them back to the more civilised purlieus of the Manor.

CHAPTER

17

The chaise in which Lady Chandross had travelled down from London, and which had also been pressed into service to convey her to the Manor, having been sent off in favour of the entire party's returning together in the Rowntrees' carriage, Eugenia found herself alone with the three persons to whom she most pressingly desired to declare the true state of affairs; but with the coachman upon the box it was obviously impossible for her to enter into explanations with them at the moment. She was obliged instead to sit in silence while the Squire and Lady Chandross had a spirited discussion, which would have degenerated into a brangle had the coachman not been present, upon where the wedding was to take place, the Squire putting forward the claims of the village church, which both Eugenia and Tom had attended from their tenderest years, and Lady Chandross holding out with fashionable obstinacy for St. George's, Hanover Square. Tom cast a sidelong glance or two at her during the short drive, as if to see how she was taking his audacious behaviour at the Dower House, but she refused to be drawn into any personal conversation until they had reached the Manor.

Once there, however, with Muffet and Mrs. Rowntree to swell her audience, she made her announcement. There was to be no engagement between her and Tom; it had all been a mistake; Tom had acted only out of chivalry in telling Lady Chandross that he had made her an offer.

"But I didn't!" Tom astonished her by saying, with some heat. "I mean, I didn't act out of chivalry! Don't be a gudgeon, Eugenia! Of course we shall be married; I should like it above all things!"

Eugenia stared at him. "But that's not

at all what you said when I asked you —"
she began, and then, conscious where her
unwary tongue was leading her, bit the
words off short.

But she had said enough to bring the
sharp-witted Lady Chandross down upon
her.

"Do you mean to tell us, you
unprincipled child," she demanded
incredulously, "that it was *you* who did
the asking?"

"No, she didn't! It was me!" Muffet
said, coming, albeit somewhat
ungrammatically, to her friend's defence.
"I — I mean," she went on, faltering a
little under the penetrating gaze of Lady
Chandross's grey eyes, "I said I thought it
would be a very good idea if — if Tom *did*
marry Eugenia —"

Mrs. Rowntree, looking scandalised,
said she had never thought a daughter of
hers would have so little delicacy.

"Delicacy be damned!" said the Squire,
who had had quite enough of the
discussion and, in his usual way, clung,
buckle and thong, to the root of the
matter. "What does it signify who asked

who, as long as the affair is settled? If Tom hadn't the rumgumption to ask the girl for himself, it's as well that his sister did it for him."

"She didn't!" Tom said indignantly, at which point a brief but spirited dispute took place between brother and sister which carried all the Rowntrees back so forcibly to nursery days that Mrs. Rowntree said reprovingly that that was quite enough, stopping herself just in time from adding that they should have no cake for their supper if they didn't behave more properly, while the Squire lost his temper entirely and said in a very loud voice that he would have no more of this.

Eugenia, deeply conscious of being the cause of all this dissension and, that she could put an end to it in a moment by agreeing to marry Tom, wished with all her heart that she could bring herself to do so; but she could not. If she could not marry Richard, she could marry no one. In desperation, she at last threw out the suggestion that she wished to become a governess, which was greeted with cold scorn by Lady Chandross, with disgust by

Tom, and with patent incredulity by Mrs. Rowntree. As for the Squire, he had gone off in a temper to his estate-room, declaring that he didn't understand modern young people and never would.

"You are a great fool, my girl!" said Lady Chandross, exasperated at last into abandoning her bored manner in favour of plain speaking. "A governess, indeed! And what, pray, do you think Cecil will have to say to that? If you won't marry Tom Rowntree, then you must take young Perry Walford. I am sure you may have him any time you choose to whistle for him!"

"No, I can't!" said Eugenia, feeling she might as well be hanged for a sheep as for a lamb. "He has already made me an offer and I've refused him!

And she fled upstairs to her bedchamber, which did no good either, however, for Muffet followed her there and under the guise of sympathising with her kept earnestly pointing out to her what a splendid thing it would be for everyone if she really would agree to marry Tom.

"I *don't* see why you won't," she kept repeating, until Eugenia finally made the fatal mistake of telling her she couldn't because she was in love with someone else.

"You *are!* With who?" Muffet demanded, wide-eyed, thus disgracing Miss Bascom for the second time that day, and made herself such a nuisance thereafter with awed and repeated questionings that Eugenia at last felt as if she would have liked to jump into bed, pull the covers over her head, and die in peace.

She had never thought a great deal about being in love before, not being romantically inclined and having read very few of the novels over which the other young ladies at Miss Bascom's had shed luxurious tears; but obviously, she thought, as she went to bed exhausted at the end of the day, it was quite as uncomfortable a matter as those marbled volumes had depicted it as being. Everyone was cross with her; Lady Chandross had assured her in the tartest possible terms that she would be taken back to London the very next day, where she would be expected to conduct herself as befitted the Earl of Chandross's ward and not in the style of some hurly-burly girl of no gentility whatever who was obliged to earn her own living; and Richard — Richard had thanked her for finding Mr. Childrey for him as politely and formally as if they had never shared a secret plan at the King's Head in Thatcham, or met in Ned Trice's little room under the leads, or eaten Old Nan's buttered eggs together in her cottage on the river.

And at the thought of those happy days, never to come again, she did pull the covers over her head and indulge in a bout of tears quite as bitter as any enjoyed by one of the long-suffering heroines whose tribulations had so affected her schoolfellows at Miss Bascom's.

In the morning, matters did not, as they usually did, seem any better to her. She was to leave for London with Lady Chandross as soon as that fashionable peeress had breakfasted and been attired by her abigail for the journey, but as this was not likely to be until an advanced hour of the morning, there would be all the Rowntrees, expressing in their various ways disbelief, disapproval, and disappointment, to be faced for what seemed to her an interminable period. She could not simply remain in her bedchamber, because Muffet and Mrs. Rowntree, and perhaps even Tom, would be certain to visit her there; so she put on her riding-dress and announced her intention of going for a short ride before she would be obliged to leave for London.

She managed to escape from the house before Muffet or Tom, who would have been certain to wish to accompany her, had discovered what she was about to do, and in a short time, by some strange coincidence, found herself approaching the wrought-iron gates of the Dower House.

Now that she chanced to have ridden in this direction, she told herself, it would be only civil to stop and say a proper good-bye to Lady Brassborough — and, of course, to Gerald and Richard if they were still there. So she turned her mare's head and trotted up the long drive between the Spanish chestnuts to the door, where she was admitted by Matthieu, who looked quite unperturbed by all the excitements of the previous day, and who informed her that Lady Brassborough was in the breakfast-parlour.

"Oh, and — and Mr. Liddiard? I mean, *both* Mr. Liddiards?" Eugenia enquired, in what she hoped was a quite ordinary voice, though her heart had suddenly begun to beat rather faster than usual.

Matthieu said that one of *ces jeunes messieurs* was already gone out, and the other had not yet risen, but as to which was which he was unable to enlighten her; and as she felt that whether Richard was away from the house or was still asleep upstairs, he was equally inaccessible to her, she followed Matthieu obediently and rather disconsolately back to the breakfast-parlour.

Here she found Lady Brassborough in an extraordinary negligee of lilac silk dripping with Malines lace, and was at once greeted with much cordiality and invited to partake of chocolate and angel-cakes.

"No, thank you," said Eugenia, which caused Lady Brassborough, who was well-acquainted with her ordinarily healthy appetite, to look at her sharply and put up her brows. "I only came to say good-bye, and to thank you again for being so splendid yesterday," Eugenia said. "Gussie is taking me back to London today, you see."

Lady Brassborough's very expressive brows again climbed up her forehead.

"So soon?" she said. "I see. Not a very romantic female, Lady Chandross, I fancy. Tearing the love-birds apart, I mean. Is young Master Tom quite desolate?"

Eugenia, who was industriously turning a Meissen saltcellar round and round as if she wished to examine it from every side, said there weren't any love-birds and she expected Tom was quite all right, only a little angry with her, perhaps, for not wanting to marry him.

"I don't, you see," she went on, still scrutinising the saltcellar with great

345

attention. "I thought I did once, and it is all my fault that he asked me, because I told Gussie he was going to offer for me so she would let me come down to Kent, and when she took it for granted yesterday that he had, he said it was so, because he is really a very kind person, and I expect he thought he wouldn't mind much being married to me. But he isn't in the least in love with me, and I —"

She stopped.

"And you are not in love with him," Lady Brassborough obligingly finished her sentence for her.

"Yes," said Eugenia in a rather small voice. "I mean, no. That is, I'm not —"

Lady Brassborough poured herself another cup of chocolate from the silver pot on the table, surveying her guest as she did so with shrewd, wise eyes.

"In point of fact," she went on calmly after a moment, "you not only are not in love with young Master Tom, you are in love with someone else. Dear child, shall I guess who it is —?"

"No!" said Eugenia in alarm, raising startled eyes to Lady Brassborough's face. She suddenly coloured up furiously. "That is, I — I am not in love with anyone!" she denied hastily. "I have decided that I shall never marry. I am going to be a governess."

"Are you, indeed?" said Lady Brassborough equably. "A very estimable occupation, I am sure, dear child, but sadly dull, I fear. I cannot but think that, if you really have no *tendre* for another young man, you would do far better to marry Master Tom —"

"No!" said Eugenia, even more violently than before.

"I see," said Lady Brassborough with great tranquillity.

Eugenia would have liked to tell her that she did not see in the least, but she had a horrid feeling that if she began to say anything at that particular moment she would disgrace herself by beginning to cry, so she went back to examining the saltcellar again. Lady Brassborough proceeded with her breakfast.

After a short time she remarked in an extremely casual voice, but with her dark, pessimistic eyes never leaving

Eugenia's face, "Gerry is still asleep, I expect. Would you like me to have him waked, so you can say good-bye to him, too?"

"Oh, no," said Eugenia. She had herself in firm control now, and spoke rather mournfully, as she was feeling mournful.

Those expressive brows of Lady Brassborough's went up again. "I have been thinking," she said after a moment, very slowly and distinctly, "now that everything has been so nicely cleared up, of going abroad for a time again, and taking Gerry with me as a sort of courier."

Eugenia said, still in that mournful, absent voice, that she thought Gerry would like that very much.

"He needs a wife, you know," Lady Brassborough continued in the same distinct voice. "Not an English one, I fancy, but a young woman with plenty of money and a Continental background, who will know how to cope with his expensiveness and his infidelities. He is a rogue, you know, but a very charming one, and I think, if he makes the proper sort of marriage, that he need not ruin himself entirely."

She paused. Eugenia, who was not at the moment in the least interested in whether Gerald ruined himself or not, became conscious of a lengthening silence and, coming to herself with a start, said she dared say Lady Brassborough was quite right.

"I am so glad you agree," said Lady Brassborough. "Now Richard, on the other hand, I should say," she went on with the same deliberation, "will need another sort of wife altogether. Someone who will be quite content to live in the country and take more interest in horses and the land than in balls and amusements and fashionable frocks — and someone, moreover, with whom he is genuinely in love —"

Eugenia pushed her chair back violently from the table and jumped up. It was one thing to know that Richard did not love her and would never wish to marry her, but it was quite another to be obliged to sit quietly listening to talk of his loving and marrying someone else.

"I — I must get back to the Manor at once," she said. "Gussie will wish to leave for London very soon —"

"You won't wait for Richard to return?" enquired Lady Brassborough, looking quite unsurprised by her young guest's sudden agitation. "He left here quite early to ride over to St. Aldwyn's and consult Mr. Childrey, and I fancy he will be back very soon."

"No — no, I can't wait," Eugenia declared hastily, feeling that if Richard were to walk into the room at that moment she would sink herself beneath contempt by bursting into tears. "Tell him — tell him I am very glad that he is to have Coverts, and — and that I hope he will be *very* happy —"

She kissed Lady Brassborough and went quickly out of the room. Lady Brassborough, left alone, poured herself another cup of chocolate, sighed, smiled, and, ringing the bell, instructed Matthieu to tell Monsieur Richard, as soon as he returned, that she would like to see him in the breakfast-parlour.

She had not long to wait. Within a few

minutes she heard Richard's step in the hall outside and in a moment he walked into the room.

"Well?" said Lady Brassborough, motioning him to a chair.

He sat down.

"It's all right, I expect," he said. He was unsmiling, his manner rather abrupt. "I've seen Childrey — there seems to be no doubt about the marriage. I expect my next step must be to communicate with Cedric Liddiard. I'll go to Canterbury this afternoon."

"You *don't* sound," Lady Brassborough said, regarding him meditatively, "highly elated, dear boy, for someone who has just come into a considerable estate."

"Don't I?" Richard got up again and walked to the window, where he stood looking out at the fine Kentish morning. "I expect I'm a bit overwhelmed; that's all."

"Overwhelmed — or merely thinking of something else?" Lady Brassborough enquired. "One so often is, you know, even at the most inopportune moments. I remember when Brassborough and I were

351

being married, all I could think of was whether Hortense had remembered to pack my chinchilla muff, which was really quite absurd of me, as it was full summer and I could not possibly need it. Eugenia rode over to say good-bye while you were gone," she added without pause, in the same conversational tone. "It seems she isn't to marry Tom Rowntree, after all. She says she is going to be a governess."

"A governess!" Richard swung round; there was a quite unreadable but definitely startled expression upon his dark face. "Why in heaven's name should she want to be a governess?"

"It is what very young and inexperienced girls always do want to be when they have been disappointed in love," Lady Brassborough explained to him kindly. "For some reason, they seem to feel it is both feasible and romantic, which of course it isn't in the least."

Richard stood there frowning at her. "Disappointed in love?" he said after a moment, abruptly. "Do you mean young Rowntree won't marry her, after all —?"

"Dear boy," Lady Brassborough said soothingly, "I gather he would be only too happy to. Eugenia is a remarkably pretty girl, you know. But there are other young men in the world, as well. Yourself, for example —"

"Myself?"

Richard looked at her, his bronzed face growing, it seemed to her, a little pale.

"Why, yes," she said placidly. "Of course I knew, when she brought you and Gerry down here, that she must be in love with one of you, but I was able to see so little of her that I really couldn't decide which of you it was until this morning. But when she greeted with complete indifference my plan to find a wife for Gerry, and almost burst into tears and rushed away from the house the moment I spoke of finding one for *you* —"

She paused, looking speculatively at Richard, who had turned away once more to the window. After a few moments he said to her in a rather harsh, steady voice, "I have great respect for your perspicacity, Lady B., but in this case I believe you are mistaken. Eugenia has never given me any indication —"

"Never given you any indication that she is in love with you? Dear boy, don't talk such fustian to me!" said Lady Brassborough with energy. "Ten to one the girl didn't know it herself until she was pitchforked into examining her feelings by all this talk of marrying someone else! I assure you, she is probably crying her eyes out at this very moment, or wishing she had the chance to, and if you do not do something quickly she *will* run away to be a governess or a lady's maid, or something equally disastrous, and end by causing the Chandrosses to wash their hands of her and ruin herself entirely." She looked at Richard for the first time rather anxiously. "Oh, dear!" she said. "I *can't* be mistaken, can I? You *do* care for her, don't you? You looked so ferocious yesterday when Lady Chandross spoke about her marrying Tom, and then so alarmingly polite, that I made quite sure —"

Richard's face suddenly cleared. "No, you weren't mistaken, Lady B.," he said.

"I *do* care — very much indeed; so much, in fact, that even having Coverts isn't worth a brass farthing to me unless I can have her there, too. If you think I have a chance, I'll put it to the touch. Perhaps if she won't take me for myself, she'll take me for Coverts —"

"Richard, Richard, don't say that to *her!*" said Lady Brassborough, horrified; but Richard was already out of the room.

"Men!" said Lady Brassborough, regarding her empty cup with dark, disillusioned eyes. "If they can't make a mull of a love scene one way, they'll do it another!"

She poured herself out another cup of chocolate.

CHAPTER

18

When Richard arrived at the Manor a quarter of an hour later, it was in the expectation of finding Eugenia about to set out for London with Lady Chandross; but such was not the case. In point of fact, even as he enquired for her of the butler, he was conscious of some sort of commotion in the house, and almost before he had pronounced her name both Mrs. Rowntree and Muffet, as if they had been on the listen, suddenly appeared in the hall with expressions of anxiety and expectation upon their faces.

"Oh — it is only you, Richard!" Muffet said in a disappointed tone as her eyes fell upon him. "Have you seen Eugenia? We

356

are in the most dreadful —"

A warning look from her mother halted her. She cast an impatient glance at the old butler, who of course knew everything that was going on but kept up a dignified pretence, for the sake of his position, of being deaf and blind as well as quite uninterested, and dragged Richard into the drawing room.

"*Have* you seen Eugenia?" she demanded then once more. "We are in the most dreadful pelter about her, because she went out for a ride early this morning and hasn't come back, and Lady Chandross wishes to take her to London and is quite certain that she has run away. Oh, Mama," she went on, turning to her mother, who had come into the room behind them and was looking at Richard in a rather bewildered way, "this is Richard Liddiard, the one I told you about that looks just like Gerry and is going to have Coverts."

Richard greeted Mrs. Rowntree, and said that Eugenia had visited the Dower House that morning, but had left, he understood, in ample time to have reached the Manor if she had gone directly there.

"The Dower House!" gasped Mrs. Rowntree. Her plump face crumpled up into an expression of piteous alarm, rather like a baby's when it is about to cry. "Oh, dear! Oh, dear! It is *just* as I feared!" she lamented. "That dreadful woman has encouraged her to run off — perhaps she will even help her to go on the stage, and then she will be *quite* ruined and Tom will not be able to marry her, though of course he will insist upon doing so, and how we are to stop him I cannot think, for even if he is not of age, he may *say* he is and people will be sure to believe him because he is so well-grown for his years —"

Richard, seeing no end to this speech in sight, cut in upon it to say soothingly that he had spoken to Lady Brassborough after Eugenia had left the Dower House, and that he was quite sure she had no more idea than had they where Eugenia had gone. He then asked Muffet, who was the more coherent of the two, whether Eugenia had given any hint that morning as to what she intended to do.

"No," said Muffet. "But I think she was feeling perfectly dreadful because we were all trying to make her agree to marry Tom and she wouldn't. It's because she is in love with someone else, you see."

"Did she tell you so?" demanded Richard, suddenly feeling as if the sun had come out with extraordinary brilliance upon a beautiful world, which was quite absurd, as it had been shining just as hard as it could out of a perfectly cloudless summer sky all morning.

"Yes," said Muffet, looking curious. "She wouldn't say who, though. I say, do *you* know?"

Richard said he didn't, but that didn't stop one from hoping.

"Oh!" said Muffet, her eyes widening. "Are *you* —? Do *you* —?"

"Yes," said Richard. "I am and I do. And don't worry, Mrs. Rowntree," he went on, addressing that agitated lady; "I'll find her if I have to scour all Kent for her, and I shan't let her go for a governess, or an actress, either." He said to Muffet, "Where would she go if she wanted to cry?"

"To cry?" Muffet, a sensible girl, first looked startled and then considered. "I expect she *might* go to Coverts," she said, after a moment. "She couldn't cry *here* because people would be sure to try to get her to stop, and there's no one living *there* now —"

But Richard was already out of the drawing room on his way to the door.

He had never seen Coverts, but Eugenia had described it for him so often, as well as its situation, that he was able to turn his horse's head confidently in the proper direction — confidently, that is, until he suddenly found himself lost in an intricate network of little lanes, most of them old drovers' tracks that had been so worn by centuries of use that they were more like cool green tunnels through the woods than proper roads. Fortunately, a small boy driving a single cow before him was able to put him right, and without loss of time he came out presently, at the foot of one of the lanes, upon the house.

There it stood, rising peacefully from the hallow of its meadows as if it had been bred and nourished by the soil just as the meadows had — the huge, rambling structure of irregular ragstone, brick, and massive, age-blanched timbers that had grown out of the original quadrangular Tudor manor. The sun was dazzlingly reflected from the leaded diamond panes of its windows. A flock of geese paraded solemnly from around the side of the house to preen themselves in the flowery heat; otherwise, nothing but peace and silence. Richard caught his breath.

After a few moments he dismounted, tied his horse to a tree, and was about to embark upon an exploration when the horse whinnied energetically and was immediately answered from around the corner of the house. Richard went round and saw Eugenia sitting on the turf under a large silver-grey poplar, to which her mare was tethered. She was so immersed in her own thoughts that she did not hear him approach, and he was able to see that she looked very woebegone before she at last became aware that she was not alone and looked up at him with startled eyes.

"*Oh!*" she exclaimed. "It's you! What

in the world are *you* doing here?''

And she jumped up so quickly that she became entangled in the trailing skirt of her riding-dress and would have fallen if Richard had not caught her.

"I came to find you," Richard said, showing no haste to let her go. "And I have. Were you crying?"

Eugenia, furiously searching in her pocket for a handkerchief, which rather obliged Richard to release her, said in a somewhat muffled voice of course she hadn't been, and, accepting the large clean handkerchief that Richard silently proffered her, mopped her telltale eyes with it and blew her nose rather defiantly.

"The reason I asked," Richard said, when this had been accomplished, "is because if by any chance it has anything to do with me, I mean the way you are feeling, you needn't" — at which point Lady Brassborough, if she had been perched somewhere above in the branches of the great poplar and thus able to hear everything that was going on, would have said, *"Men!"* in the same scornful tone she had used that morning in the breakfast-parlour of the Dower House and washed her hands of him entirely. "I mean," Richard went on, feeling even with his own imperfect masculine comprehension of what a love scene ought to be that he was making an appalling mull of it, "I should like it above everything if you would marry me and come back to live here at Coverts again —"

Eugenia looked not at all cheered by this offer, and tears began instead to well up in her eyes again.

"Oh, Richard!" she said. "How very k-kind of you! But I couldn't possibly let you make such a s-sacrifice!"

"A sacrifice!" said Richard, looking thunderstruck. "But it wouldn't be! What put such a cork-brained idea into your head —?"

But before Eugenia could reply, the clip-clop of a horse's hooves trotting smartly up the drive interrupted them, and around the corner of the house came a very sedate gig, driven by a plump, scholarly-looking clerical gentleman who gave the appearance of having very little notion where he was going, being content to leave such mundane affairs to the discretion of his horse while he concentrated his mind upon more important matters. At sight of Richard, Eugenia, and the latter's mare, the horse stopped, instead of going round to the stable-yard, which had obviously been the clerical gentleman's intention insofar as he had one, and the clerical gentleman came out of his meditations and saw them.

"Eugenia, my dear! And Gerald!" he exclaimed with a pleased expression upon his face, at the same moment that Eugenia, starting forward, cried, "Cousin Cedric! What are you doing here?"

"I have come to make my quarterly inspection," Mr. Cedric Liddiard explained, climbing down from his gig without making the least provision to prevent his horse from wandering off in any direction it pleased. Richard, coming forward, took the reins and tethered the horse to a tree. "Such a weight upon my shoulders, my dear," continued Mr. Liddiard, "for one *does* feel dreadfully inadequate when Willcox — an estimable man, I am sure, but so apt to expect one to understand drains — goes through estate matters with one. Gerald, my boy," he went on, turning politely to Richard, "how are you? Have you been — I *do* seem to have heard something — getting yourself into trouble again?"

"It isn't Gerald. It's Richard," Eugenia said. "He looks just like Gerry, but he isn't. He is Cousin Charles's son, and Cousin Charles and Susan Justis were married by Mr. Childrey at St. Aldwyn's, so he is your real nephew and is to have Coverts."

Mr. Liddiard looked bewildered.

"It's quite true, sir," Richard said. "I might say I was sorry to dispossess you, but it would be a lie. I never set eyes on this place until five minutes ago, but I know already that it's where I belong."

"Yes, yes, of course it is — since you are poor Charles's son," Mr. Liddiard said, rather distractedly. "Dear me, dear me! This will take a bit of getting used to, you know! Still you can't think what a relief it is to me, my dear boy! I *don't* understand the land and never have, and yet one's obligation to it — bless me, I can scarcely believe in my good fortune! Shall I really never be obliged to come here again?''

''Not unless Eugenia and I invite you to — which I hope we shall do very often, sir!'' Richard said, looking amused. ''We are going to be married, you know.''

''Are you, indeed? Dear me, this is indeed a day of happy surprises!'' said Mr. Liddiard, beaming upon Eugenia. ''How splendid for you, my dear! I know how attached you have always been to Coverts! And now you will be coming home again.''

''But I'm not —'' Eugenia began, looking indignantly at Richard, for it was more than should be expected of any girl, she felt, to sacrifice the dearest wish of her heart twice in one day. ''Richard is only being k-kind —''

''She hasn't quite got used to the idea yet, you see, sir,'' Richard said blandly. ''And as she is expected back at the Manor and it is apparent that I still have some explaining to do, perhaps you will excuse us for the present? When I have seen her back to the Manor, I shall return and we can have a talk, if that will be convenient.''

''Oh yes! Dear me, yes! Highly convenient, and very proper!'' Mr. Liddiard agreed cordially. ''I shall tell Willcox all about you, and he will show you over the estate, I am sure! He will be very pleased, you know, very pleased! I expect you understand all about drains — *and* crops, *and* cows —''

Richard said not all about them, perhaps, but what he didn't know he would be happy to learn, and untying Mr. Liddiard's horse from the tree, helped the happy clerical gentleman into his gig, which then proceeded on its way around the house to the stable-yard.

As soon as it had disappeared, Richard turned to Eugenia, but before he could speak she backed away from him, both hands out to prevent him from approaching her.

''No, Richard — *please!*'' she said rather desperately. ''I know you are only doing it to be k-kind, and — and not thinking in the least of yourself, just as you were when you stopped that horrid young man from shooting me at the Dower House —''

"So far is Richard from being kind," he said, advancing ruthlessly upon her and taking her into his arms in spite of her attempts to ward him off, "that he will probably beat you if you persist in making that idiotish statement. My darling, *sensible* little widgeon, has it never occurred to you that I have been in love with you ever since I first set eyes on you in the King's Head at Thatcham, or I should never have allowed you to cozen me into entering upon that outrageous masquerade at Mere in the first place?"

"But you — but you never —" Eugenia managed to protest, but very ineffectually, for Richard was holding her so close that she was sure he could feel the wild beating of her heart.

"I never told you so?" Richard completed the sentence for her. "The devil of a coxcomb I should have been, to ask you to marry a penniless bastard, who couldn't offer you so much as a name!

And by the time I discovered that my circumstances had changed, *you* were engaged to Tom Rowntree.''

''That,'' acknowledged Eugenia, hanging her head, ''was a mistake.''

''I have gathered as much.''

''And,'' she went on, struck by an interesting thought, ''you can't offer me one now, either, Richard. A name, I mean — at least not a new one, because if I marry you, I shall still be Eugenia Liddiard. Or would I be Eugenia Liddiard Liddiard?''

Richard said that as far as he was concerned she would be Mrs. Richard Liddiard, which was good enough for him, and at that point his impatient feelings got the better of him to the point that even Lady Brassborough, had she been looking down upon the scene as before from the poplar's upper branches, would have been more than content with his performance. Eugenia, emerging radiant and breathless from an ardent embrace that Lady B.'s most romantic leading man would have found it difficult to improve upon, gazed up at him with starry eyes.

"Oh, Richard!" she said. "I think — I really *do* think that you may be in love with me, after all!"

"*Think!*" said Richard. "*May be!* Good God, my girl, what must I do to prove it to you?"

But at this point Lady Brassborough, being a discreet woman when circumstances demanded, would no doubt have flown silently away from her perch in the poplar tree, remarking, "Yes, that is *much* better," to herself in an approving tone, and allowing the rest of what seemed to be shaping into a highly satisfactory love scene to be played out undisturbed in the golden brilliance of the sweet-scented June day.